OF
MOURNING
DOVES AND
HEROES

Ross Tarry

Published by Kieley Publishing
St. Michael, MN 55376

This book is dedicated to my wife Bunnie,
and to the memory of my great friend
and mentor
Maureen LaJoy.
Nearly every Monday morning
she would call and in that
sweet voice of hers encourage me to write.
Her legacy lives on through us.
Also to my fellow writers
Judy, Janet, Lyn, Joannie, Sue, Judd,
Laura, Larry, Linda and Genny
at the Maple Grove Community Center who
continue to urge me on.

Ross Tarry

Of Mourning Doves and Heroes

-1-

Carmine Valentino, lay belly-flopped over his redesigned child's wagon struggling to lift his head and couldn't. His thick arms hung useless, the back of his scarred and callused knuckles, lay limp in the grass. His short bone-thin legs hadn't moved on their own in over thirty years.

When the man in coveralls and scuffed sneakers knelt beside him, Valentino managed to get his head up for a brief second. Seeing who it was, his eyes showed a thankful pleading and his struggling stopped.

The coveralled man slipped a rope through the wagon handle. Then laying a hand on the old man's back, he leaned close and spoke calmly. "Make your peace, *Amico Mio*. You know what must happen now. You remember how it was in the old days."

The old man strained and bucked, his shoulders coming off the worn pad on the plywood deck of the wagon for a split second. His white head of hair came around, eyes wide. He tried to shout but only a grunt from the back of his throat came out. His torso rose with one deep strained breath. His face reddened, the powerful neck muscles twisted the head violently side to side lifting his trunk for an instant, then he fell back with the whoosh of escaping breath. His legs remained still.

The man in coveralls stood up and stepped backward, trailing the rope down the driveway and along the edge of the road until the water filled ditch was between him and the man face down on the wagon. Twisting his hand in the rope, he dug his foot into the soft earth at the edge of the asphalt and pulled. And the Radio Flyer that had given Carmine Valentino the freedom to move about the yard and among his precious flowers for over half his life transported him down the slope to his death.

Of Mourning Doves and Heroes

-2-

Titus V. Closson, the town marshal, has a bearish quality. In the way he moves, quick and agile in spite of his size and age, (fifty-nine), and in the way he takes in his surroundings, not in anticipation of danger or trouble, rather, a total awareness of his immediate environment.

The morning sun, cresting the wooded hills, spilled in a warm yellow column through the bedroom window. Titus pulled his belt tight and patted it into the loop then picked the small gold star from the cluttered dresser and pinned it to his crisp, blue cotton shirt. Slipping his watch over his wrist he saw it was after eight. Have to remember to pick the laundry up from Martha's, he thought.

He gave the mirror a cursory glance to check his gray, short trimmed hair, twisting to catch his reflection through the many yellowed newspaper clippings of a young girl in gymnastic clothes taped around the edge and down the center.

He walked to the window and stood in the yellow sunlight of the late summer morning and looked out on the back lawn. Blackbirds picked through the damp grass. In the corner of the yard a white squirrel scampered along the telephone line to the house. Clusters of red berries hung from the young Mountain Ash by the back fence. I'll stop on the way back from the county seat, he thought. Maybe Martha's picked some squash.

Titus flipped the comforter over the sheet on the bed, sat and pulled on his black low-heeled boots, then took a second to check the moisture in the bushy pot of sweet basil on the nightstand with his finger before rising to close the window. He knew it would rain before evening. It had every day for a week.

He steadied himself against the dresser and rubbed the tips of the boots on the back of the dark slacks then clipped the holster with the 9mm Beretta and the pager over his belt.

When he walked into the kitchen Ann Marie was standing at the counter with her back to him. "Good morning, Sunshine," he said. At her elbow lay the unopened morning paper.

"Morning, Dad." She glanced around quickly. "I see you're dressed for work. Not going for your run this morning?" She spoke without turning as she fixed her breakfast of toast and tea.

Titus flipped open the paper and read the headlines: TODDLER SURVIVES FALL FROM SECOND FLOOR BALCONY

"I have to go in to Sweet Springs later. I got a letter from Wiggins yesterday, the Thompson kid's trial is set. I hope it's not one of your cases?"

"No," she replied. "It's Jerry Gatkin's case."

"Good," he nodded. He also would stop at the printers and cancel the campaign posters if they weren't already printed. He had let himself be pushed into the idea of posters and regretted the decision the instant after he'd said okay. A piece of red cardboard with his name printed on it, tacked to a slat and stuck in the center of someone's lawn seemed more than a bit lurid to him. He would tell her over dinner this evening.

Titus dropped the paper on the table and got a cup from the cupboard. "On the way back I'm going to stop at Martha's and pick up the laundry. And some fresh picked squash if it's ready. Do you have anything to drop off?"

Ann Marie was dressed for work in a white silk blouse, a charcoal skirt, nylons and, as usual around the house, no shoes. Her long brown hair came to the center of her back and was brushed to a sheen. As she buttered a slice of toast she scratched the back of her ankle with her toe. "No thanks, I did some laundry last night, but if you're still in the court house at noon, I'll treat for lunch."

Titus watched her. Ann Marie looked exactly like Sandra had in their early years, a long time ago, when his wife was young and healthy. He felt the pang of love, and loneliness that sometimes struck him. A knot tightened in his throat. He swallowed. He had been a widower for seventeen years. Just him and Ann Marie now. Next to his marriage to Sandra, Ann Marie was the best thing that had ever happened to him.

She turned and saw him staring, leaned over and gave him a peck on the cheek. The feeling of loss quickly turned to pride, as it always did when he was around his daughter. Last April he had watched her prosecute her first case, moving around the courtroom with nearly the ease and confidence of a seasoned prosecuting attorney. She was a natural.

"You're on," he said, pouring a cup of coffee. He had lifted the hot cup and blew across the top when the pager beeped.

When he hung up the phone Ann Marie was watching him, her brown eyes wide with curiosity.

"What was that about?"

"The sheriff's dispatcher. A call about a drowning at the Valentino house."

"Valentino?"

Of Mourning Doves and Heroes

Titus reached into the cupboard for a plastic mug; dumped the coffee in and popped a cap on. "That white house on the S- curve on Develin Road."

She was shaking her head, her eyebrows arched gracefully over her soft brown eyes.

"The paraplegic on the wagon," Titus answered.

"Okay. Yeah. Fill me in at lunch. I'm in a hurry."

In the driveway Titus slapped the flashing dome light onto the roof of the blue sedan and backed into the street. The lettering on the side door read Lawrence Town Marshal.

* * *

Lawrence, once a hamlet full of promise. Just one day's travel west of Sweet Springs by stagecoach had failed in mid-life to grow into the commerce center envisioned by its founders. Its existence had started at a shallow crossing on the Rock River and expanded west along the territorial road for one mile before it gave in to the oak and aspen hills.

Today it is a town of two story clapboard houses with crumbling foundations and small ramblers with single car garages. Where the green grass of front yards ends at the gray asphalt of the road. Where men of long tooth and plaid shirts stir morning coffee and talk of game scores in Bud's Tavern. Where graying matrons compare liver spots and brag up grandchildren in the dining room of the Grand Hotel across State Highway 12, Main Street.

The Grand is a three story red brick building with a covered wooden porch--white railings and white spindles with green ivy cover the porch roof which frames the third story windows. The flashing light that sways gently over the highway at the center of town, and makes the traffic on First Street stop, is the controversy of the day: Petition the State to change it to a four way stop or remove it.

The bank is the second red brick building and the town hall the third red brick building. A Tex-Oil station stands next to an implement dealer with green farm machinery parked on the sidewalk and Bennet's Grocery & Cold Locker, a two-story frame structure with huge plate glass windows in the front. And the park is shaded by ancient maple and elm trees, where every November on Veteran's Day everyone sips hot cider, an ox is roasted and grandkids wander at the rusting gray hulk of a World War I tank.

As Titus came through the S-curves he recognized the county ambulance sitting just off the road in the concrete driveway. Two men stood on the front lawn near the deep drainage ditch that ran alongside the blacktop road.

He eased the car to a stop just past the driveway, careful not to pull too far onto the soft shoulder lest the car slide into the water-filled ditch. On the lawn, at the feet of the two paramedics, he saw the body of a man sprawled face up and an overturned child's wagon. He switched off his roof light and stepped out to see a Sheriff's cruiser come screaming up the road, screech through the S-curve and pull onto the soft mud of the shoulder just short of the driveway. Titus recognized Cliff Hensley, the young Deputy from town. His older sister had been one of Ann Marie's young school friends.

"Morning, Charlie," Titus said, looking from the body, to the wagon, to Charlie, to the ditch. He noted a slipper on the grass near the body and another at the edge of the brackish water. "He was in the water when you arrived, I see."

The other attendant was watching the approaching deputy.

"Yup," Charlie said. "The deceased and that wagon there."

"He was still on the wagon?"

Charlie glanced down at his wet pant legs and muddy shoes. "The body had slid forward, half in, half off the wagon. Only the feet were sticking out.

Pete and I both had to go in. I pulled the wagon out first then we drug the body out by the feet."

"Did you try to---?"

Pete was shaking his head. "The guy was in the water too long. He was already cold."

Titus knelt at the body. The man had been in his seventies but by no means frail. His clothes were soaked and Titus could see that although from the waist down he was scarecrow thin, the upper half of the body was very muscular. The matted fine white hair and gray stubble of whiskers were flaked with debris from the bottom of the ditch. The eyes and nostrils were caked full of the muck.

Titus pulled the bottom lip down with his finger. There was mud between the inner-lip and Gum; fibers of weed and black flakes in the teeth. It was as if the man had been planted headfirst in the bottom of the drainage ditch.

"Well," Titus said, getting to his feet. "Looks like he was breathing when he went in, at least. Cliff, have the dispatcher call for the coroner."

Titus' attention shifted to the strangely modified wagon then to the white clapboard house. He walked across the lawn and up the drive toward the neat, well-kept house with low green shrubs along the front and a tall wide Maple shading the southwest corner. A late model sedan sat in front of the single car garage. A concrete sidewalk bordered by mounds of beautiful orange and

Of Mourning Doves and Heroes

yellow Marigolds led from the driveway to a wood-plank ramp at the door of the rear entrance to the house. He stopped at the foot of the ramp. The air was heavy with fragrance. He inhaled the pleasant scents then walked to the back. The rear yard was ablaze with blossoms from a huge variety of flowers growing in beds laid out in straight, one-foot wide strips that crossed back and forth across a lush, perfectly edged green lawn. In the center of the yard was an elaborate birdbath made of small field stone in various shades of granite gray. The old guy got around pretty good for a man in his condition, Titus thought.

He walked up the ramp and reached for the knob and the door opened. Titus' mouth fell when he recognized the woman standing in the doorway dressed in a short sleeve white smock, white blouse and white slacks.

"JoAnna?"

She seemed shaken. "I was watching through the front window, Ty. What a terrible way to die."

He studied the woman standing in the doorway. He hadn't seen her since Wagner's funeral. She was a lean, pretty woman. Always had been, he recalled with a faint flush he hoped didn't show. The dark chestnut hair he remembered was almost all gray, and there were fine lines in the thinning skin around her eyes and at the corners of her mouth. Her sharp cheekbones were dotted with brown freckles, the only makeup she wore was a light coral lipstick.

"May I come in, JoAnna?"

"Oh, Ty. I'm sorry." She pulled the door open and stood aside. "I just can't believe something like this could happen."

Titus stepped inside. The kitchen smelled of toast, butter, and eggs, reminding him he hadn't had breakfast. "This is quite a set up, JoAnna. You worked for Valentino?"

As he spoke he looked around. The kitchen was equipped for someone with Valentino's abilities. Low cabinets, the counter top and sink high enough for a wheelchair to slip under. To the left of the arched doorway to the living room a power hoist hung from a swinging I-beam attached to the top of a steel pole secured upright in the corner. The sling hanging from the hoist swung over a wheelchair. The only thing ordinary in the room was the table with two chairs under the open window facing the walk and the garage. A huge colorful bouquet of Zinnias sprouted from a blue vase in its center. Across the room was a small slanted table with a telephone, several phone books and a vinyl three ring binder filled with paper. Tacked to the wall beside a pencil holder was a typed sheet of paper covered in plastic. Through the doorway Titus could see a television, its silent screen alive with brightly colored shapes moving across a brown, green, and blue map of the United States.

JoAnna shut the door behind him. "I work for Homecare Services. In-home nursing and nutritional care. One meal a day and I lay his medication out. From eight to eleven, three hours a day, six days a week. I really feel bad about this, Ty. I've been on the phone. We have a list of calls to make if anything ever happens."

"May I see the list?"

JoAnna pointed. "The open folder over there. My supervisor in the office. Emergency home and pager numbers."

Titus reached for the note pad in his back pocket and the pencil in his shirt. He recognized the county hospital in Sweet Springs. Along with the other numbers with names behind them. When he finished writing he put the folder down and turned back to JoAnna. His mind drifted back to when they were younger before he met Sandra and before she met Wagner. She was a junior and he a senior in high school. He shook away the memory. Too many years ago.

"You arrived at eight then?" he asked.

"A few minutes before. When I turned into the driveway I saw something in the water in the ditch next to the culvert. I recognized his slippers. Carmine always wore them."

"Carmine was Mr. Valentino's first name?"

"Yes." She paused, letting Titus finish his notes. "I tried to pull him out, Ty. The bank is quite steep and the wagon wouldn't budge. He was just too heavy. I started to go in the water---. It looked deep. I was afraid I wouldn't be able to get out. So I left him there and ran back to the house and called the emergency number."

Titus could hear the guilt in her voice. "You did the right thing," he reassured her. He looked down, her shoes were wet and stained. "With no one else around, you could have been stuck in that ditch until someone drove by and noticed you."

Her gaze fell to the floor and she shook her head slowly from side to side. "I just wish I could have done something more. It felt wrong to just leave him there. Who would have thought that wagon would roll down the bank into the water like that?"

Titus reached out and put a reassuring hand on her arm. The instant awareness of the silky smoothness of her skin startled him. He pulled his hand away, too quickly. "You s'pose I could see the rest of the house?"

She led the way through the archway into the living room. The room was smaller than the kitchen with a plate-glass window facing the front. And it was sparse; on the right, against the wall the silent, flickering television, a Maple rocker with a folded bath towel for a seat pad, a small table in front of the window with cut flowers and two brass floor lamps, one in each corner along the front wall.

He followed her across the room, through another doorway and into a bedroom with windows facing south and east.

"Mr. Valentino must have been in fairly good shape. Do you know how old he was?"

"Seventy-eight last month."

"His health?"

"He had a heart condition. He was on Propranolol and Warfarin. Could he have had a heart attack?"

Surveying the room, Titus shrugged. "I don't know." So this is where Carmine Valentino lived, Titus thought. A large unmade bed filled one corner. There were dozens of green, blooming plants on stands and small tables under the east window. A wooden table strewn with paper, bookcases filled with books, a desk and a computer fit neatly in the room. JoAnna touched a button on the wall and the door to the bathroom slid open. Titus nodded his head. He was impressed. Beside the usual fixture was a sink high enough to slide a wheelchair under, a handicap equipped ceramic tiled shower, a power hoist, and a contraption for exercising.

"Tell me about him. What kind of man was he?"

"He never talked about himself. Just friendly talk. Always said good morning, thank you and good-by. Polite, you know. Sometimes idle chit-chat while he ate, mostly about flowers or the lawn. Didn't like things done for him, though."

"Hmm." Titus looked around the room then went back into the bedroom. His eyes fell on a yellow legal pad full of penciled writing. "Looks like he spent most of his time in here."

"He might have. But in the mornings when I was here he was always outside. I think he might have stayed in the house only that one time when it had rained all night and the ground was so wet he couldn't push himself around on the wagon."

Titus crossed the room, ran his hand over the top of the computer monitor, and looked through the window onto the back yard. "He sure seemed to get around okay, though I don't think I ever saw him in town or anywhere other than in this yard."

His thoughts turned to the only way he had ever seen Carmine Valentino, occasionally in a wheel chair but mostly face down on that specially designed child's wagon with the wide tires pushing himself around the yard with his hands. Sometimes with a woman nearby.

JoAnna followed Titus back into the living room. Through the large window Titus saw an unmarked black van slowing in front of the house. "The coroner is here, JoAnna. I better get out there." He paused in thought. "I know I've seen another woman around here, his wife?"

"I wouldn't know about a wife, but I understand he had a nurse for years, up until four weeks ago. Not from any local service, someone he had hired himself. When she left he contracted with us."

At the door Titus turned to her, his hand on the knob. "There is really no need for you to stay, JoAnna. If whatever you need to do is done, you could go."

"Thank you, Ty."

She was standing beside him, her scent blending with the bouquet coming through the window.

He turned the knob slowly, stopped. "If there is anything else I need I may have to call you."

Her eyes smiled. "Yes," she answered without hesitation.

* * *

Titus righted the wagon and dragged it back up the slope away from the ditch then approached Dr. Jerry Henderson in the driveway while the two attendants and the Deputy slid the loaded gurney into the back of the coroner's van, locked it to the floor and slammed the door closed.

"For your report, cause of death is accidental drowning. Autopsy, Marshal?"

"I wouldn't think so, Jerry. Not unless there's a request from the family. They've already been notified, so if there is a request you should hear today."

Cliff Hensley waved and headed back to his cruiser. Titus waved back then watched the ambulance beep, beep onto the asphalt and follow the cruiser down the road.

Titus' attention was directed to the house by the bang of a door. He turned and watched JoAnna walk to her car. You could tell a lot about a person by the way they lived, especially if they lived alone. JoAnna exuded self-confidence, a knowledge that she did not need the help of another in coping with everyday life. He didn't like dependent people. He saw dependency as a self-centered handicap, had seen it used as a crutch and as a means of controlling others. Valentino had made the best of his solitary, confined life. That was evident in the house, equipped superbly for a man with his disability. In the immaculate lawn and the abundant flowers. Whoever this Carmine Valentino was, he had found a quiet, efficient, and effective way to get through life. From the looks of his home he was at peace with himself, which is really about all you can ask.

Titus watched JoAnna back her car around and come down the drive and stop beside him. She handed him a folded sheet of stationery. He opened it. It contained her address and telephone number.

"I would like it very much if you would call, Ty."

"I will," he said, feeling the same flutter in his stomach he had felt in the kitchen of the house. "And we'll have dinner," he added, aware of his own smile as much as hers.

He stepped back and watched her car turn onto the road, glide through one curve then disappear around the other. He looked at the note in his hand and the address written in large eloquent pen and felt a quickening of his pulse. He folded it once and slowly creased the edge with his thumbnail. A squirrel chattered in the trees across the road. "Yes. I think I will," he said softly, and tucked the slip of paper into his shirt pocket.

Ross Tarry

-3-

T he menu was small. Titus ordered onion soup with no cheese and their Famous Crusty Bread, and water. Ann Marie ordered the seafood salad and hot tea without looking at the menu. She leaned forward, her right elbow resting on her small black purse lying on the table. "Okay, what happened this morning?"

He thought of JoAnna and for a brief second he felt a flush in his face. They always talked well together, he and his daughter, but the subject of JoAnna would wait for further developments.

Her eyebrows arched. "Valentino. The Gangster."

"The what?"

"The gangster. That's what we called him in school."

"Why?"

She flipped her hand. "Just school yard talk I would imagine. You know how it happens. One kid with an imagination comes up with a tale and soon it's all around the school."

"Well, what was the story?"

"If I remember right, he was supposed to have been some kind of big time mobster shot up in a gang war, and gone into retirement. Pretty exciting stuff for us kids." She sipped her water and looked around for the waitress. "I remember a few of the boys took to peeking in his windows expecting to see machine guns."

Titus put his hand to his chin and stared down at the table, this was all new to him.

"Well what happened this morning?" she asked.

Titus' mouth curled and he shrugged. "He rolled down a bank into the drainage ditch in front of his home and drowned."

She looked at him expecting more.

"It got away from him, I guess. The wagon. You've seen him, belly down on that strange looking wagon of his, pushing himself around the yard with his hands."

"Sure."

"Well, this time he got too close to the bank and couldn't stop or maybe slid in the damp grass. Whatever happened, the paramedics found him in the water when they arrived, too dead to help."

Of Mourning Doves and Heroes

The waitress came with the tea in a china cup and chipped saucer. Ann Marie pulled it close, stirred it twice, lifted a spoonful to her lips and blew softly across the top. "Are you going to pick up your posters today? I'm sure they're ready."

His eyes were on his daughter's hand as she sipped the tea from the spoon. "I've been thinking I would pull out of the race. I've only got a little over two years left before I can draw pension. I don't need this kind of campaign. Lawrence is a small town. A village. People are taking sides. That's not necessary. It's not good. Feelings will get hurt. And for what. You know as well as I that the only reason Tony DeGosi wants the job is to run for sheriff in two years. So he can say he's held elective office. I'm just not sure I want to be a part of this."

"Dad." He could hear the opposition in her voice. "What makes you think he will win? You can't throw sixteen years away just because that little turd has some grand scheme. Show him up for what he is."

Titus felt his lips twitch with a smile. She was always his greatest champion, encouraging him. It was something they did for each other, out of father-daughter loyalty.

He tightened his mouth. "Sunshine, watch what you say." He feigned caution, his eyes searching around the diner.

Her dark eyes sparkled with anger, her jaw set tight, she looked across at her father. When she spoke her voice had fallen one notch. "He is a turd. He's a sorry excuse. Six months in the State Patrol and he claims to be a crime fighter. If it wasn't for someone, and I'd like to know who, we would know why he resigned the patrol. I'll bet it would be very interesting."

"I know. I know." Titus waved his hand. He liked her bite and had to force himself to keep from smiling. "He's a two bit politician."

"He's a bull-shitter. Just like his father."

The waitress came, set a brownstone bowl of soup and a wooden board with a small golden loaf in front of Titus. A minute later she returned with Ann Marie's order.

Titus broke off a hunk of the warm bread, dipped it into the soup and slipped it into his mouth then reached for his napkin. "Anthony's okay. He may be a bit pompous but so what? Most of the people in this town and many of the local farmers have loans through his bank. I've had loans there for most of twenty years. And he's carried many a hard-lucker, a few longer than he should have."

"I know. But I still don't like him."

They ate in silence for several minutes before she spoke again. "Well, I still would like to know what happened in Jefferson City, why he got booted off the Patrol, and I'll bet that's what really happened. If I went up there I wonder where the tracks would lead."

Titus looked up, popped a bite-sized piece of sopped bread into his mouth and wiped his fingers. "That's what bothers me," he said, mostly to himself. "Tracks."

Ann Marie was watching him. "What?"

He held another hunk of bread between his thumb and forefinger suspended in the warmth of the bowl. "Tracks," he repeated. "The ground was soft. We've had a shower almost every evening. And there were clear tracks in the grass made by the wagon leading into the water. And tracks where the attendants scuffed up the lawn getting the wagon and body out. Wouldn't you think there would be other marks coming down the slope? It's not a long or particularly steep incline, ten or twelve feet, but you would think that a man who's only way of getting around was his arms--- Ann Marie, he was a powerful old man. His arms were as big around as your legs. You would think he would have tried to stop the rolling wagon. Turn it or throw himself off. At the very least he would have dug his hands into the ground in trying to stop. There were no signs that he did."

"Heart attack or stroke?"

Titus popped the sopped bread into his mouth, and swallowed, "Could be. But he was not totally incapacitated when he went into the water. He struggled some after he went in. Not much, but enough. The eyes and nose were full of dirt and the mouth, he must have ate half a pound of the bottom of that ditch before he died. Even an old man without the upper body build he had would have struggled more."

He patted his chin with his napkin. "But he never used his arms."

Ann Marie set her fork on her plate and pushed it to the side. "Well, I'm sure there's a very logical explanation. By the way. I have a dinner date tonight, Dad. I won't be home 'till late."

Titus showed surprise. She hadn't dated much since she stopped seeing Cal Hampton over a year ago. "Good. Someone I know?"

Although a part of him secretly trembled every time she mentioned a date, fearing that all too soon the day would come when she would leave forever, he encouraged her. People needed to be with their own social group. She was young, had desires, social and physical. His body shook with a chill, he hoped it hadn't been obvious.

"Sandy Baker," she replied.

His face winced with disapproval, his ears turned red. "Sunshine!"

She laughed a short laugh. "He's all right, Dad."

"He's a used car salesman!" Titus spat the words.

Of Mourning Doves and Heroes

Her grin dimpled her cheeks and her eyes sparkled. "He is not. He manages Lake Tower Apartments for Doc Adams."

"I know what he does for a living. He's been bragging he found a career that suits him. He's been there for a whole two months. But he's still a car salesman. Too damn slick to trust."

The muscles in her face drew her lips into a tight pucker but her eyes still sparkled. "Dad," she admonished. She turned her wrist and looked at her watch.

"All right, all right." He pushed his bowl away and slid his chair back. "I've got to get going, too."

At the register he paid the check, left two dollars for the waitress, slipped his arm around his daughter's waist and they walked out the door. On the sidewalk she slipped from his arm, took his hand, gave it a squeeze and asked, "Where are you headed?"

"Back to Valentino's place to look around."

Her hand was still holding his. He gazed down into the face of the one who had been the worry of his life for so many years. "I'm sorry about giving you a hard time."

She was smiling. There was nothing in the world that could melt him as quickly or make him feel as good as her smile, it filled him with warmth and brought a tightness to his throat that made him feel delight as well as anxiety. He started to speak another word of caution but checked himself when he felt her squeeze his hand again.

"I'm a grown woman, Dad. When are you going to stop worrying about me?"

"Never," he answered, in a whisper.

"Okay. I give up. Now, I've got to go." She turned her cheek to him. He responded with a kiss.

*   *   *

Titus pulled off the road in front of the driveway and stopped. He got out, circled his car, crossed the corner of the lawn and squatted beside the overturned wagon. It was a child's wagon, originally. Red with a low, steel box. That was the only thing about it that hadn't been modified. The carriage had been reinforced with steel angle iron and it had wide pneumatic tires. The tongue had been shortened and bent upward like a ski so it would slide along the ground without digging into the earth, then a cross bar had been welded on the end forming a "T". Valentino, lying on his stomach on the deck, could turn the wagon by pulling the handle to the side.

In the grass beside the wagon lay the padded wooden platform that fit on the top. The tattered and stained padding, still wet from the ditch, may once have been a quilted comforter. Titus stood and lifted the wooden top on end. He guessed it to be about fifteen inches wide and maybe four and a half feet long. On the bottom, a rib of wood had been screwed around the edge to hold it in position over the wagon box. He carried it to the car and slid the board in. Then set the brown bag of squash on the seat beside the basket of neatly folded clothes and went back for the wagon. He had to move the first-aid kit and the plastic case with the shotgun from the trunk to the front seat before he could fit the wagon in.

He closed the trunk and walked to the point where the lawn began the slope to the water-filled drainage ditch. On his hands and knees he followed the wagon tracks down the shallow incline. Alert for any sign of what he felt should have been there. Some sign that Carmine Valentino had tried to stop the roll to his death. The sod had not been disturbed until he got near the water where JoAnna and the attendant's struggle were obvious. He pushed himself to his feet, brushed at the grass stains on his knees, then walked back to the crest of the incline and onto the driveway. He could see the divot where one tire had ridden up onto the grass. He knelt on the concrete drive facing the road and fingered the indentation the tire had made. Then searched until he found the mark made by the other tire. The left tire had made a deeper, more distinct sliding mark. He stood and looked toward the garage, and attempted to piece the events together.

Valentino must have come down the drive at a pretty good clip then cut onto the lawn at an angle, he reasoned. That would account for the left tire digging into the edge of the lawn. Which means he came down here to the road for a specific reason; he wasn't just working on the lawn.

His eyes traced the path to the ditch. The water. "The culvert is plugged. There's no water on the other side." He spoke the revelation aloud.

On the left side of the driveway the grass-lined ditch was nearly dry, only a trickle ran from the steel culvert to dampen the washed sand at the mouth. Two wide deep tracks made by an ATV cut from the road down into the soft bottom. A lighter trail came in from the lawn side. On the other side of the drive the tracks came out of the water and onto the road just above the culvert.

The service door of the garage was unlocked. Titus pushed the door open enough to see the hand tools hung low along the wall. He grabbed a hoe and a steel rake and trotted back down the driveway. After several minutes of probing with the rake he pulled up an inner tube, a big one from a truck tire. Immediately he could hear the rush of water flowing from the other side. He turned and watched. Water gushed in a thick brown stream cutting a trench into the sandy bottom, washing away the ruts made by the ATV.

He watched the surge of water until it slowed to a hose sized stream. Then he spent the next thirty minutes in the slick muddy bottom of the ditch with the rake collecting the rest of the items that had blocked the opening of the steel culvert. Only to wash through with the torrent of water, the remnants of a wax milk carton, a tattered plastic grocery bag from a convenience store, gum wrappers, candy wrapper, thick blue-black clumps of soggy newspaper and gobs of stringy grayish slime that was once bathroom tissue that clung to the bowed-over grass like soured cream.

Titus laid everything out on the concrete drive and put the tools away. Then backed his car around, spread his poncho on the front seat and loaded the articles he had collected, wishing as he did for a pair of poly-gloves. He then walked back to the house, to the hose faucet. He squatted and washed the mud from his hands. Halfway back to the car he stopped and looked around. Carmine Valentino lived in this town, on this road, in this house for twenty-five years and I never knew him. I wonder who did?

He turned his back to the house and gazed out over the road and yellow highlights of the trees across the road. There were no other homes in sight. He tucked one wrist under his arm and put his other hand to his chin. Somebody must know something about the guy. A person can't live in one spot for so many years and not get to know anybody well, no matter how private a life they lead. He pulled his top lip between his teeth. It seemed he had just described himself.

Titus turned the car onto the road toward town, then stopped and backed slowly along the ditch until he could see where the water line stopped. When he was across from the orchard he saw the ATV tracks running along the bottom of the ditch to where the water had been, then turned up and onto the road. And, where at least once the tracks had gone up the other side. He sat for a moment then turned the car around and slowly followed the tracks up the road. Maybe whoever had been running the ATV saw something.

-4-

The silver-cased travel clock on Titus' desk read four-fifteen when his call was answered. "Jennifer, this is Ty Closson. Is the sheriff in?"

"I'll check, Marshal." The click of the phone in his ear and the silence seemed to draw the heavy, sweet smell of honeysuckle through the open window of his first floor office. The chair creaked back; , he swiveled and turned to look out. The air smells different in the fall he thought. The crisp fragrance of autumn flowers and the stale, mellow aroma of the changing leaves settled in on the land like a heavy cover of antique fog. The smell of age, of death and the end of a life cycle. Beyond the horizon loomed the steel-gray cloud of a stark winter.

He inhaled deeply and Ray Watkins came on the line. "What's up Ty?"

"Ray, it's that Valentino thing this morning. Do you think you could get someone from your lab over there? Some things just don't fit. I think we should find out just how the guy died."

He explained about the tire tracks and his collection of trash now spread out on the desk that the lab crew could pick up. He was about to call Dr. Henderson and ask him to do an autopsy on the body. The sheriff agreed and hung up.

Titus fingered the phone button and dialed the coroner's office.

"Sorry, it's too late, Marshal," Jerry Henderson said. The words came too fast. Titus looked at the clock and wondered if he had caught him leaving for the day.

"The body left for Jefferson City over an hour ago. I received a call before noon saying a car was on the way, and would there be any problem. I said no. That is what you said."

"You're right. But things aren't adding up."

"Like what?"

"Just little things. Can we get an autopsy done in Jefferson City?"

There was a pause on the line followed by a sigh. "With consent of the family or is this official?"

Titus thought a moment. He already had the Sheriff's lab involved. Might as well make it official. "This is official, Doctor."

Of Mourning Doves and Heroes

The Doctor's words ran down as he spoke. "Then I need an authorization."

"Can you get things started while I dig up the forms and get them to you?"

Titus didn't know Dr. Jerry Henderson very well, but the man's attitude was irritating him. "Maybe if I have Sheriff Watkins call you," Titus said finally, indicating his annoyance by his tone of voice.

"No need, Marshal. I'll call the mortuary and notify the Cookton County Coroner's office, if it isn't too late. It is four-thirty, you know. And I'm sure they'll require the authorization. I'll have to fax that to them."

Titus felt a flash of heat slip from under his collar. "It's four twenty-five, Doctor, and I'll be in your office with the paperwork by five."

The seconds of silence on the line told Titus he was not making a friend. "Okay, Marshal. I'll be waiting."

Ross Tarry

-5-

Ann Marie was in her robe and barefooted. "What's up for today, Dad?"

Titus tipped the coffee pot and poured his cup full before he spoke. "Two AM is awful late to be out."

She set the toast on the counter and turned to him, her lips drawn tight. "Daaad!"

"I know. I know. You're a grown woman. I understand that, but that Sandy Baker is as full of shit as a Christmas goose."

She stood glaring at him, her eyes spitting, the stern expression on her face unchanging.

There were so many things that reminded him of her mother. The way she stood her ground, the fire in her eyes. The tilt of her nose. It would be fifteen years in November since Mo's death. Damn the cancer.

Ann Marie broke the stare just long enough to find her toast and tea, then crossed the room and sat at the table with her legs crossed before her eyes fell away from him.

"Honey ---"

She interrupted, her voice calm. "Dad, who I see is my business. What time I come home is my business. I know you worry, and I love you because you do, but please---."

Titus set the cup on the counter and leaned back taking a deep breath, the creases at the corners of his mouth smoothing into a serious expression. "Father's give advice, Sunshine. And sometimes express opinions. That's the way it is. That's what I do. And I will for as long as I'm around." He paused for only a second before continuing. "You are not required to heed it of course, all I ask is you give it some thought. Sometimes people overlook things if their focus is on something else. What they miss could be important."

A smile flicked across her lips and a flush rose in her face, then both quickly vanished and she took a bite of toast. "Do you remember Todd Peabody?" she asked, setting her teacup down.

"No."

"Well, we worked together on the school paper. I called him yesterday. He's a reporter on the Jefferson Sentinel."

Titus' brow curled. "So?"

Of Mourning Doves and Heroes

"So I asked him to find out what happened with Tony De Gossi and the Patrol."

"We are not going to start throwing mud, Ann Marie."

"We are not going to. But you can't just sit back and let him slander you. If there was something illegal or improper going on the voters have a right to know."

Titus said nothing. How could this happen. Fourteen years as Town Marshal, friendly if not friends with everybody, and now this. Name calling. Innuendoes. All for a do-nothing, pension job. I should have stayed on the Jefferson City Force. I could be retired with a decent pension by now. The memory of a terrified ten-year-old Ann Marie the night he came home from the hospital with a knife wound in his back, only two weeks after putting her mother in the ground came back to him. No, returning to Lawrence had been the right thing to do.

A curious look came over her face. "Dad?. You okay?"

Her voice snapped him from his reverie. "What?"

"Are you okay?"

"I'm okay." They had always been truthful with each other. "It's just," Titus paused, thinking. "For some reason I've been thinking of your mother lately."

The look lingered for a moment then faded slowly from Ann Marie's face. She uncrossed her legs and rose, scraped crumbs from the table into the saucer and set her dishes in the sink. "You sure you're alright?"

Titus responded with a nod.

"Okay," she said, then gave him a one-armed hug and under her breath said, "You were right about Sandy. I can't tell you about it, it's too personal, but you were right."

*   *   *

"Linda, I'd like to see Anthony if he's not busy."

"I'll check Marshal." The middle-aged woman lifted her phone and punched a button.

A moment later Anthony De Gossi came out of his office. "Titus. Good to see you."

"Good morning, Anthony." They shook hands.

"What can I do for you?"

Titus' eyes flickered around the bank.

"Come in the office." Anthony reached for Titus' arm and guided him around Linda's desk and into the plush office. Anthony De Gossi was a tall man, as tall as Titus, but thinner and a few years younger. A full head of silver hair brushed to a sheen with not a strand out of place, framed a square and delicately featured face. His skin, though thin and wrinkled around his starched collar and across the back of his hands, was tanned. Dressed to the nines in a gray worsted suit, the man looked like a healthy, middle-aged movie star. Anthony circled his desk to the window and motioned to a leather-upholstered chair. Titus sat, his eyes going to a framed picture of a younger man carrying a gun and holding a wild turkey.

"The best time of the year, Ty. Cools down just enough in the evening for a light jacket."

"Yes. If it would only stay like this."

"What can I do for you?"

Before Titus could answer Anthony raised his hand. "Wait. First I have to say I hope there are no hard feelings between you and me because Tony is running against you."

A dozen seconds passed before Titus realized Anthony's statement was meant as a question. "No, no hard feelings."

"Good," Anthony rushed on. "I don't know why the boy wants to be Marshal. I mean no offense Ty, but the job is a no money job. Tony could do much better for himself here in the bank."

Titus shifted in the chair and crossed his legs. "The young people have to go their own way, just like you and I did."

"I guess," Anthony said, moving his head from side to side. He pulled his chair out and sat, his arms flat on the desk with the red stone in his ring glistening in the sun. "Okay, what can I do for you?"

"Nothing of a personal nature, Anthony. How well did you know Carmine Valentino?"

"Too bad about Carmine. A real shame. He was a decent guy though sometimes he came across as a bit of a curmudgeon."

"You knew him well then?"

Anthony's fingertips came together and went to his lips. "For many years. He'd been a customer here at the bank almost from the day we opened. Why?"

"Monday morning two young boys on their way to school saw what they described as a fancy black car parked in his driveway. They took a close look at the car, you know how boys are, but couldn't see any name on it, just numbers. I remembered you have a Mercedes E320. I thought it might have been yours."

"Yes. I was there. He'd called last week about rates on a loan for some home improvement. Not much. Three thousand dollars. I told him considering his age maybe he should think about just using some of his savings." Anthony chuckled softly. "He jumped all over me, told me my job was to give him the information requested, that he would make his own decisions. And anyway he planned to outlive me."

Of Mourning Doves and Heroes

Anthony De Gossi's smile vanished and his face turned serious. "I remember laughing and telling him he probably would."

"He called the next day and said my interest rates were to high. Too God damned high, is what he'd said. Said he had put the figures in his computer and even figuring in the tax break, had determined it would cost him less to just draw the funds from a savings account. He asked if I would set up a separate checking account and bring him the paper work. I did. Monday morning."

"He had a substantial amount of money then?"

"Well, he had several accounts with us. Most of his transactions were done through the mail but occasionally I would stop at the house, maybe three or four times a year. Ty, why the questions? Is something wrong?"

"I really don't know. It's just I don't think he died the way it first looked. At first glance it had seemed the wagon just got away from him and rolled down the embankment into the water. But I don't think that was the case. He may have been sick, or possibly a stroke or heart problem. In any case an autopsy will tell. One more thing, do you know anything about the nurse? Her name?"

"Carol. I knew her. A hard old bitch. It surprised me when he told me she had quit. They must have had some pretty lively conversations."

"You wouldn't have any idea how I could get a hold of her."

"No." Anthony shook his head. "I only knew of her through Carmine."

Titus stood. "Thanks Anthony. I won't keep you any longer."

They shook hands across the desk.

"Not a problem, Ty." Anthony came around the desk and put his hand on Titus' shoulder. "Tell Ann Marie hello for me. I haven't seen her around since she got that great position in the county attorney's office. You've a right to be very proud of that girl, Ty."

"I am, Anthony," Titus said, in the doorway. "I am."

Walking across the lobby Titus wondered just how proud Anthony was of his kid.

Titus left his car parked off the edge of the road and walked up the driveway past the two gray sedans and the blue and white van with the Sheriff's gold seal on the side that was backed up to the rear door of the house.

Sheriff Raymond Watkins, his gold shield hanging from the breast pocket of his blue blazer was standing in the doorway facing in. He turned when he heard Titus call out. "You get a copy of the autopsy report?"

"Yes. Thanks for faxing it over, Ray. I see Henderson had the Cookton County Coroner send it to you instead of me. I guess I ticked him off last evening when I asked him to stay late and do his job."

The sheriff's mouth twitched, and his head jerked slightly. "That's too damn bad."

Titus looked around, drawn to the rows of blossoms by their heavy fragrance. A bluebird flitted around the stone birdbath then settled on the back fence with its mate. Too much activity to feel safe. Wonder who's going to take care of their piece of paradise now?

"Cause of death was drowning, but what do you make of the Dantrolene in his system?" In the west, the gray and white puffs of clouds were assembling for their evening attack.

"According to the coroner that's heavy stuff and he had enough in him to take a healthy man down."

Titus followed the sheriff through the entryway into the kitchen. A woman in a light blue smock was going through the cupboards, listing everything on a clipboard. Another technician was on his knees with a brush and a tin of a white powder dusting the back of one of the kitchen chairs.

The flowers on the table caught his eye and his mind reeled back in panic. Where had he put the slip of paper with JoAnna's number on it? His dresser?

"Something wrong Ty?"

Titus put his hand to his forehead and brushed it back over his head to his neck. "Just thinking, Ray. Overdose of his medicine?"

"We haven't found any Dantrolene yet. There wasn't any with his medications."

Titus snapped around, surprised. "Then how did it get into his system?"

The sheriff lifted his hand and he shrugged. "That would be good to know. The lab went over the lawn and the ditch last evening, before dark, then sealed this place up for the night. They've been here since about eight. We haven't found anything obvious. We're just listing everything."

Titus stood transfixed, one ear on what the sheriff was saying. There had never been a murder in his town, not in modern times anyway. A couple of suicides, an auto accident or two, a hit and run. "Valentino was murdered, Ray."

Ray Watkins had his hands jammed in his jacket pockets, he nodded. "All we have to do now is figure out how, why, and who. Like I said we went over the ditch and front yard real good. We got a few good impressions. Now I'm trying to decide if I should call in the State Lab boys to sniff the house with their vacuum. Probably a waste of time, the murderer may never have set foot in here."

Of Mourning Doves and Heroes

Titus crossed the room to the vanity, the plastic vials of medication were gone and the tray where he had seen the capsules was empty.

"That's all been boxed for the lab. I should have a complete report tomorrow. I'll send you a copy."

"Who prescribed his medication?"

The sheriff pulled a notebook from the inside of his coat, and flipped the pages. "A Doctor Borgland. Filled by Riverside Drug. Different dates. None over sixty days old."

Titus nodded. "Borgland's the new Doctor in town. I haven't met him yet. Wanna come?"

"Nah. Just tell him one of my people may be stopping in. I'll stay here for a while. Then I have to get back to the office."

Titus hesitated in the doorway. "I'm not stepping on your toes am I?

"This is your town, Ty. The county will work with you on this. We'll back you up but you're the lead. Just be aware of your jurisdiction and keep me informed." The sheriff winked and a smile tugged at the corner of his mouth. "You're the one up for re-election."

Ross Tarry

Of Mourning Doves and Heroes

-6-

Titus left the car at the curb, climbed the wet stone steps of the brick fourplex and pulled the heavy glass door open. Inside, above the mailbox tagged J. Simmons, was a call box. He pushed the black button and waited. A fine rain was falling from a pewter sky, he brushed the drops from his jacket sleeve.

A woman's voice came over the box. "Yes?"

"JoAnna. It's Titus."

"Titus. I will be right down."

His stomach fluttered and his eyes darted to the street then the car. He hadn't felt this uncomfortable in years.

Through the inside door a crimson carpeted stairway led up, another down. He caught his reflection in the glass, snapped the toothpick from his mouth, and glanced around frantically for someplace to toss it then jammed it in his pocket when he saw satin slippers coming down the steps.

JoAnna was wearing a scarlet silk blouse that cut in under her breasts to her waist and a chain with a silver pendent. The black cotton slacks were just tight enough over her hips to reveal a still firm figure. A knot twisted in his throat when he saw her radiant face. She was as glad to see him as he was to see her.

She pushed the door open. "Ty," she beamed.

"I hope I didn't disturb your evening, JoAnna."

"Oh no! I'm sorry to keep you waiting, Ty. Come in. Come in."

Her smile plunged into him and he felt his heartbeat quicken.

"We'll have some tea." She held the door open with one arm. Titus sucked in and squeezed by close enough to inhale her powdery fragrance but careful not to brush against her.

"Follow me," she said. "Careful you don't slip with your wet shoes."

He wiped his feet and followed her up the steps unable to keep his eyes from the silver ankle bracelet that danced lightly around her left ankle.

Inside he eased the door closed behind him and took in the impressive apartment. The carpet was plush ivory and there were Degas prints hung on the wall. A glass and chrome dinette was placed in a square of glistening honey-blond parquet. A long contemporary oyster shell sofa, two matching easy chairs and a glass coffee table sat in the corner next to the French doors that opened onto a narrow deck. Next to them rested a maple rocking chair with a silver, satin cushion.

JoAnna took his jacket, hung it in the closet and gestured toward the sofa. "Please sit down, Ty." She disappeared around a divider into the kitchen. "Tea or coffee?"

"Coffee would be fine." while Titus sat at the table he heard a cupboard door slam and water run.

"I'm afraid instant is all I have."

His stomach was fluttering, and the thought of coffee brought a sour taste into his throat. "That'll be fine JoAnna."

He stared through the glass doors that opened onto a narrow charcoal gray deck glistening in the drizzle. Beyond the green mowed perimeter was a flat marsh with clusters of cedar and high, browning grass and beyond that a deep green wall of Tamarack. On the deck, blossoms drooped in the box of flowers and water splashed from the wooden rail and ran down the glass.

JoAnna served coffee, tea and a dish of cookies from a silver tray, and sat down across from him.

"Thank you." Titus tasted a cookie. "Delicious."

JoAnna slid the teacup toward her. "You sounded serious on the phone. Is it about Carmine?"

"He was murdered, JoAnna."

She sucked a breath of air, the back of her hand went to her mouth and she paled. "Murdered?"

Titus nodded and withdrew a pad from his breast pocket and flipped it open.

"Why and how? Who would do such a thing?" Her eyes grew wide, her hand still at her lips.

"I don't know. All we know is someone, or something caused him to go into the water. It was not a simple accident," he said. He drew a pen from his pocket. "Did you know him before you went to work for him?"

"No", she answered. The color that had started to come back vanished and she turned white as snow. "Ty, you don't think that I--" She stopped, not finishing the sentence.

He hesitated for a second, felt a stab of heat burrow into his chest then reached out to touch her arm. "No, JoAnna. We just need to find some answers."

Her eyes closed quickly. When she opened them her color was coming back, and her face opened into a smile. "Well, thank goodness."

He was suddenly aware her hand had fallen away from her face and he was holding her wrist. He could feel her pulse pounding beneath his fingers. He let go and turned in his chair and referred to his notes. "The Coroner's report fixed the time of death at seven-thirty." His eyed were drawn back to her. Inside he fought to keep his mind on the investigation. He cleared his throat. "Yesterday you said Carmine was always outside by seven. There was black dirt under his fingernails. He had, evidently, been working in the garden before he died. Do you remember seeing anyone on the road? A car, or someone walking?"

She touched her finger tips to her lips. "There isn't much traffic by there. The road ends at the new Highway eighty-seven cutoff, now." Her eyes shut for a second. "No, nothing."

"Valentino ever mention anything about boys on an ATV?"

"Yes! Monday morning I think. Evidently they had driven across the lawn. That was the only time I had seen him angry. He said he would be ready for them next time."

Titus finished writing and looked up. "I talked to the boys' mother yesterday afternoon. Her sons drive the ATV to school and back. Valentino was laying in wait for them Monday afternoon. Told them the next time they came across his lawn he was going to call the Town Marshal."

"I guess he could be a bit crotchety."

Titus picked up his cup from the saucer, sipped and set it gently back. "How about visitors?"

She tilted her head up. "Yes. A young woman one morning, late. He was in his wheelchair out in the garden. They never came in the house and I never went out. She was there when I left. He never mentioned her name and I never asked."

"When was this?"

"Oh," JoAnna paused, "Several weeks ago. No. No." She slapped the table. "It was my second day there. I remember, because I was late leaving. I stayed to do some charting and the next morning Carmine scolded me in his way. He said he didn't expect me to stay after eleven. That there was nothing so important that it couldn't wait until the next day."

"So that would make it when?"

"On a Tuesday, the third week of August."

Titus flipped to the back cover of his note pad, "August, twenty-first," he said, then flipped the pages back and made a note. "What did she look like?"

"Oh, Ty. I don't know." He watched her hand go to her chin.

"Was she young? Old?"

She raised her teacup and held it to her lips with her fingertips. "Yes. Yes, young. And she had long dark hair. She was dressed nice, I remember. In a gray blazer with the wide cuffed sleeves."

Titus' mind wandered as he watched JoAnna. There was an energy in her silver green eyes, a vitality that unsettled him. He forced himself to look away.

"And she carried a brown valise."

"A what?"

"A brown valise. You know. A small leather travel bag."

"Anyone else?"

"No. Not while I was there. But one day about a week after the woman was there he asked me to make fresh coffee before I left. That was all. I assumed he was going to have company."

The muscle in the back of his right leg began to pulse. He shifted in his chair, crossing his legs. "Could it have been the same woman he was expecting again?"

"He never indicated who it might have been."

The apartment grew quiet while Titus paged through his notes. "According to Doctor Borgland, the nurse's name was Carol Bates. Do you know anything about her?"

"Carol. Oh yes. I remember him mentioning her. And I got the impression they had not parted on good terms."

"Like how?"

"Well, he said he wished she had left a long time ago, that he didn't understand why he had put up with her abuse for so many years."

"He used the word abuse?"

"Yes."

Titus penciled a note and slapped the notepad closed and slid it in his shirt pocket. "I've got some phone calls to make. Carol Bates is supposed to have moved to the Jefferson City area and I'd like to talk to her."

He moved to go. "Thank you for the coffee." He pushed himself to his feet and looked down at JoAnna. An expression of sadness blinked across her face, then was gone, like a fleeting dark thought.

"You're sure about Carmine?" Her eyes were on him.

Titus nodded. Then JoAnna was up, getting his jacket. "I hope I was of some help, Ty."

"You were." He pulled his jacket on and started the zipper. "Did you ever hear anything about Carmine Valentino being a retired gangster?"

She grabbed his hand. "No! Was he?"

For a moment his gaze dropped to their clasped hands, his throat fluttered. "I don't know. I had never heard that either, until yesterday morning, but it seems that was the story around the school. At least when Ann Marie was in school."

She was still gripping his hand. Her fingers were thin but firm. Their eyes met briefly, his stomach hardened. He half-turned toward the door. What am I afraid of? She's as beautiful as ever. She is interested. She has already said yes to dinner. She's just waiting for me to ask. And after all, we were lovers, once.

Titus turned the knob and the door clicked open. JoAnna pulled his hand gently, turning him back to her. The space between them was charged, stars danced in her eyes. "Ty," her voice was soft, and matter-of-fact. "I have had a reasonably happy life. I retired from nursing two years ago, after thirty years and when Wagner retired we were going to visit Robert and Lea and our grandchildren in California."

Her voice wavered, "When Wagner died it was like someone put my world in a box and shook it, then poured it out. My life didn't look or feel anything like it had. It was all there, just all mixed up. Even the things I recognized didn't seem the same. Memories that had always made me happy, brought tears, what had brought peace of mind, now brought spitting anger. But the worst was the quiet." She looked away. "I am sure you know these feelings."

Before Titus could answer she turned her face up and continued. "That was two years ago and in that two years I have grown to cherish my independence, but there are a few things in this life that I miss that I would like to do again, and a few things I've not done that I would like to try."

She paused for an instant and her voice dropped one note. "Things that are better done with a companion."

A red hue flushed her cheeks then waltzed across the static space between them to light a blush on his ears. "You have always occupied a special place in my heart, Ty. I am sure you know why. And when I saw you walking up the driveway yesterday, even though it was under a terrible circumstance, I could not help the delight. This might be bold, Ty, but in my seasoned years I have learned to speak out. I would very much like to see you."

Titus' heart thudded in his red ears, his neck grew hot. He was hearing her words on a level that seemed an arm length away. He could feel the charged touch of her hand holding his. There was something passing between them through that clasp, an energy that sent a spark through his loins and weakened his knees. Her eyes widened slightly and her lips parted and he knew she was feeling what he was feeling. His head was moving back and forth in disbelief, marveling at the effect she was having on him.

She jerked her hand away, and he heard a short disappointed groan. First he was startled, then he smiled. He reached for her hands and cleared his throat. "I wasn't saying no, JoAnna. I was just thinking about, well---. I was just thinking."

Of Mourning Doves and Heroes

Her smile gradually came back.

He shuffled from one foot to the other. His throat was so tight he could barely get the words out. "I will call," he squeaked. "Soon."

*   *   *

Titus dropped the phone in its cradle with a grimace. Philip Sanders wasn't home and he hated talking to those machines. He spun his Rolodex then picked up the phone again. Leah Massley answered. "Leah, is Dallas home? It's Titus Closson."

He laughed softly to himself. "Okay. I'll hang on."

Titus liked the wife of his old beat partner. She was a born mother hen, especially with Dallas. When he had been the one to get knifed in the back in that garbage-littered alley in the Jefferson City flats instead of Dallas, she had mothered him like her own son. There hadn't been a happier woman in the world than Leah at Dallas's retirement party.

He could hear her in the background explaining in a voice loud enough to be heard over the entire block who was on the phone. "And hurry, it's long distance!"

A door banged, and Dallas Massley's voice came on the line. They talked for a long time and Titus could tell when Leah must have walked into the room, Dallas's tone softened. It must be wonderful sharing the last portion of your life with a woman who cares so much. And for one brief instant Leah wore JoAnna's face.

"Dallas," Titus said, shaking himself back to the reason for the call. "I need a favor. I need to locate a woman by the name of Carol Bates. She was, or is, a nurse. Until six weeks ago, she lived in Sweet Springs and worked for a man named Valentino here in Lawrence. Yesterday morning he was found dead, drowned in a drainage ditch in front of his home. It was no accident; he was murdered."

"And she's here in Jefferson City?"

"Supposed to be. She broke her lease according to the manager of the building in Sweet Springs. He said he let her off the hook because she had lived there for twelve years. Before she left she told him she had some business in Jefferson City that would take a few weeks but she would be where it's warm before the first cold spell."

"Well if she's here I'll find her, Ty."

Titus had no doubt that if she could be located Dallas Massley could do it. He had acquired an amazing number of friends and acquaintances during his years on the street and he held a chit on most of them. He thanked Dallas and gave him his office and home number and asked him to call as soon as he had something, then he called Ray

Of Mourning Doves and Heroes

Watkins. The sheriff was gone for the day, but had left a message for him that nothing unusual had been found in the house, the prints collected were being run through the system, and he had decided against calling in the state lab crew. Titus thanked Linda and asked that she have Ray call him in the morning.

Ross Tarry

-7-

T itus came in through the back door, slipped out of his running shoes, stopped at the fridge for a glass of juice then headed for the shower. He turned slowly in the hot spray letting it wash over his skin like silk ribbons on edge. The two-mile run usually cleared his mind, flushed out yesterday's accumulation of waste and left him with a clean sense of today. But not this morning. This morning, in his mind's eye, JoAnna had accompanied him. Matching gait for gait confidently at his side, or gliding along at arms length in front, her face radiant. Saying words that could mean she was assenting to intimacy if he was interested. He reached for the shower valve and turned the hot side down.

When he came back into the kitchen he was shirtless, shoeless, and wiping his hair with a large bath towel. Ann Marie was in her robe talking on the phone. She saw him standing in the doorway. "He's right here, sheriff."

She held the phone out. "Don't leave until we talk, Dad. I've got to get into the shower," then she handed him the phone.

"Ray, did your people see Doctor Borgland?"

"Yes. He said the same thing the coroner said. With the amount of Dantrolene found in the body, combined with his normal medication; he could have gone into a coma and died any time."

"That's what he told me. One more thing, Ray. What do you know about Carmine Valentino being a mobster?"

"Nothing. Where did you hear that?"

"Kid talk, around the school a number of years ago. Probably nothing to it but nobody seems to know much about the guy."

"I'll check around."

"Thanks, Ray."

"By the way, Ty, Ann Marie was just asking me about Tony De Gossi. I gave her the name of a man at the academy. I know she is doing it for you, just caution her to be careful. She has a career to think about, too."

"I will, Ray. Thanks again."

Titus poured a mug full of coffee, tossed the towel around his shoulders, went out the back door and sank into a lawn chair. A dozen Starlings glided in and settled onto the lawn, their colors glistened a deep violet in the bright morning sun. He watched them picking at the grass, all in unison, all oblivious to his presence. When he lifted his cup to his lips they spooked, sailing up over the wire fence to join hundreds of others rising from the brown grass of the vacant field, circling into a twisting black band, then sweeping away toward the river.

He rubbed his eyes and sipped again at his coffee. Thoughts of JoAnna had kept him tossing all night. His attention focused on his hand. He could still feel her touch, a tingling that raised the hairs on his arm. The surprise wasn't so much that she had awakened him so, it was that these stirrings of desire were so vivid, so intense. He had dated, occasionally. Amanda Blake the waitress at the Moons in Riverside. And there had been others in the seventeen years since Sandra's death. Yet nothing that made him feel what he was feeling now, vital, lusty, and most frightening, an eagerness that turned every idle moment to thoughts of this woman, thoughts that made his hands sweat.

A noise jolted him and he turned to find Ann Marie standing beside him with a curious look on her face. "Well, you weren't here, that's for sure."

A sheepish grin distorted his face sinking dimples deep into pink cheeks before he caught himself. "No. No, I guess I wasn't."

In the passing seconds of awkward silence the smirk on Ann Marie's face changed to a worried look. "Dad, is something wrong?"

"No, Sunshine. It's nothing." He pointed to the folded lawn chair leaning against the house. "Get the chair and sit. I want to run some things by you."

She drew her robe tighter around her. "Let me feed my birds first, then give me a few minutes to dry my hair and get dressed."

She held the seed cake in her fingers. Lifting her arm to the two mourning doves waiting on the telephone wire, she called the names she had given them. Titus watched them swoop from the wire, and a moment later the two powder gray birds plopped onto the window sill, waiting hesitantly for Ann Marie to set the food down. Talking softly Ann Marie gently laid the seedcake on the sill steadying it lightly with her finger tips. The two doves strutted along the sill, heads bobbing with each waddling step, to take the food from her as they had nearly every day since spring. First one pulled a seed loose, then the other, until they had picked the last seed from her fingertips.

Ann Marie stepped back, still holding the doves in gentle conversation. Their bobbing heads intent on their benefactor until they sensed there was no more food. Then one followed the other in a flutter across the yard to the maple. "They'll be gone, soon," she said. Her words were painted in sadness. "Can you imagine what it would be like to leave your home every year of your life for four months?"

"Wherever it is they fly to, it's also their home, too, remember?"

"I suppose."

"And when they return next March they'll settle right in like nothing's changed. But it will have changed."

"Like how?"

"Oh, the trees. The flowers. Things always change. What if something should happen and when they come back, we aren't here?"

It was these occasional melancholy moods she slipped into that he had always found unsettling. He had never found a satisfactory reply. "Go," he said. "I'll fix your tea."

The sun had crept twenty minutes higher into the blue, clouded sky. Titus had dressed, heated water for tea, and fixed toast with thick layers of peanut butter. He had just arranged their breakfast on a fold-up table between the lawn chairs when Ann Marie returned. She was in her usual Saturday morning dress; one of his shirts, a plaid flannel with the sleeves rolled up, jeans, and white canvas shoes. She had pulled her hair back into a long ponytail that, in the sun, glistened with highlights of auburn as she moved. She slipped an arm around him and gave him a one-armed hug then tipped up on her toes and kissed his cheek. "I'll refill your cup," she said.

They started their meal discussing the sights and smells of autumn. By the time Titus' coffee had cooled, Ann Marie's cheerful face had grown serious. "Sheriff Watkins said the Valentino case has been classified as a murder. You're both sure that it was?"

"Yes," he replied. The tone in his voice hardened. "And Ray also said that you asked him about Tony De Gossi's time with the Patrol."

She broke her second piece of toast in half and tore off the crusts. "Yes I did. He gave me the name of a man at the Patrol Academy."

Titus held the last of his toast in his fingers. "What happens if you find nothing, and it gets out you've been all over the state digging for dirt?"

Her face shifted into a grimace as she stared at her father. "Dad, De Gossi's been calling you a incompetent dinosaur and saying that you and the sheriff are trying to make the accidental death of an old man into something it's not. Just for the publicity."

Titus' mouth fell. "You heard all this! Since yesterday?"

"Yes. He also hinted that there was a lot of "shady goings on around here" that need looking into."

Of Mourning Doves and Heroes

A flush crept from his collar and the toast crumbled through his fingers and dropped to the table. "The only thing shady is that little shit and what's going on at the Sun Dancer." His chest filled drawing his shirt tight, then sank with a heavy sigh.

"Where did you hear this?"

"A reporter from the Palladium called me yesterday afternoon. He had just interviewed De Gossi and wanted a comment. The interview will be published in the Monday paper. I told him no comment." Her gaze fell away.

Titus' eyes were on his daughter. The straight line set of her mouth and the twinkle in those dark eyes said she was holding something back. Titus knew the look. He had seen it every time she felt she had the edge and was about to pounce. He waited for the twitch at the corner of her mouth. It came. He smiled to himself and reached for his cup.

"Well I did say that Tony De Gossi was a slimeball pervert who would sell his grandmother's walker for scrap. But I didn't say that was ready for print. Yet."

Titus' face turned soft, his lips parted, he shook his head slowly. "Just be careful, Sunshine. You have a career that's much more important than mine."

She laid her hand on his. "Don't worry about me. I'm all grown up, remember?"

Grown Up? he thought. Yes, I know you are. But then why is it every time I look at you I see my little dark haired girl? And every time you turn those eyes on me I feel so much larger than I really am?

Titus nodded, his mouth pursed in reluctant agreement. He rubbed his fingers together, sticky with peanut butter and crumbs of toast.

"I'll bring you a wet cloth," Ann Marie said, sliding her chair back. She gathered the dishes and tossed the crusts of toast toward the back fence where she knew the albino squirrel would be waiting.

"Thank you," replied Titus. "And then I'd like to bounce some ideas off you."

"The murder?"

"Yes."

"Oh, good."

The white squirrel had snatched the crusts of bread and scurried up a nearby maple. Down the street a lawn mower sputtered to life. Titus wiped his hands with the warm wash cloth. Across from him Ann Marie set her teacup in the saucer, propped her elbows on the table and her chin in her palms. "Okeeey, Marshal. Wa'cha got?"

Titus' eye brows arched, his eyes rolled and he shook his head from side to side, then he dug the note pad and pencil from his pocket. Tearing a blank sheet from the back and wetting his thumb he flipped forward until he found the beginning of his notes. "Carmine Valentino, a man in his seventies, paralyzed from the waist down is found drowned in a dammed up drainage ditch. He had lived actively but quietly, in the same house for over twenty-five years. The people in the area knew him as not being overly friendly, though no one had ever had any trouble with him. He seemed to live comfortably, he had two accounts at the bank, but there is no sign of significant wealth. Nothing in the house seems to be missing, in fact he seemed to have had little of value. He was on Propanolol and Warfarin, drugs to control his blood pressure and heart condition. A drug called Dantrolene Sodium was introduced into his body.

"Introduced? How?"

"Don't know. The autopsy revealed no needle marks. According to the report the combination of drugs could make him lethargic or kill him depending on the dosage. Twice in the past two months Doctor Borgland was called to his home. Some kind of seizure. But Valentino had recovered by the time the doctor arrived."

Titus paused to mark in the note pad, then continued. "He had a nurse of twenty-two years who suddenly quit and disappeared. And the rumor on the playground is he was a mobster in his younger days." Titus set the note pad aside, twirled the pen in his fingers a moment, then across the top of the blank sheet he wrote, "What is the motive?" and underlined it. Halfway down the page he wrote, "How was the murder committed"?

He looked at his daughter. "There are a few other things we know. We know he had a small run-in with two boys on a four-wheeler the day before he was killed. I talked to the boys and their mother yesterday after school. She stuck up for her sons. Seems the ditch had been filling with water lately and they had crossed his lawn to get around the water rather than going into the road. He caught them and gave them a what for." Titus paused for a second and put his note pad down. "The reason the ditch was full of water was because the culvert under the driveway was dammed up with bags of garbage. I picked the dam loose. There was an inner-tube, but it was mostly poly bags and wax milk cartons, things that would resist being dissolved in the water."   "You're saying the culvert was deliberately plugged."

Titus' nodded. "Knowing the water would keep rising as long as it kept raining. It was almost over the road."

Ann Marie's head, still resting in her hands, bobbed when she talked. "So the drug subdued him enough to get him into the water, yet not enough to render him unconscious."

Of Mourning Doves and Heroes

"That's the way it looks to me. Even going so far as to have two trial runs, possibly to get the dosage just right."

"But why not just kill him outright?"

Titus shrugged and was interrupted by the phone. Ann Marie stood, "I'll get it."

Titus continued writing.

"Dad. It's Dallas Massley," Ann Marie called from the kitchen.

When Titus hung up he tore off the address he had scribbled on the phone pad.

Ross Tarry

-8-

Titus eased the car to the curb and scanned the south Jefferson City neighborhood. "According to Dallas the landlord said she seldom goes out," he said to JoAnna.

On the right was thirty-four twenty Stevens, a huge three-story Early American home with heavy coats of peeling white paint and a sagging porch. The disrepair and the row of mailboxes on a board beside the door signified the fall of the stately mansion. Across the street, in front of a square, red brick, two-story building in a row of identical buildings, a young boy and a young girl sat in bare dirt behind a wire fence playing with an overturned wagon. They looked up briefly then returned to their task of spinning the wheels.

Titus reached for the door latch. "Would you prefer to stay here?"

"Oh no," JoAnna replied. "I wouldn't be of any help if I stayed here, now would I? I will tell you that I am a bit nervous, though."

"You stay to one side. If it looks like she is going to cooperate I'll introduce you as my associate. There shouldn't be any need to explain further."

Titus pulled the latch and hesitated in thought, one foot planted on the asphalt. He hoped that bringing JoAnna along wouldn't turn into a big mistake. His plan was to spend the day together interrupted by twenty minutes of official business interviewing Carol Bates. The inference of being on company time would afford them time together without the aura of intimacy that always seemed to permeate their time together. It had worked, somewhat.

Leaving the car, he stretched the two-hour drive from his muscles, reached in the back seat for his sportcoat and pulled it on. The snowy, silver-lined clouds overhead amassed into a bank of dirty gray in the west. He twisted the button of his jacket closed. JoAnna was waiting on the sidewalk. As they walked together up the steps to the door a ghostly panic settled in his mind as he thought of the possible physical dangers he was putting JoAnna in.

The mailboxes were black. On the one numbered 202 the name Bates was printed on a slip of paper and taped to the front. The door creaked when Titus pulled it open and they stepped into the once ornate vestibule. The flower patterned wall covering was yellow with age, a glass chandelier hung from the ceiling. 101 was stenciled on the painted brown door on the right. Straight ahead was another door marked 102. On the left, worn carpeting covered the steps of the stairway, and the top of the varnished handrail was rubbed black.

Titus led the way up the stairs. He knocked on 202. The hall was small. To his back was a window. On the right, next to door numbered 201 was a pair of mud-caked hiking boots. JoAnna crowded behind him. He knocked again.

He heard the latch click, and saw the knob turn. The door opened to the length of a chain and a woman's face. "Carol Bates?" Titus asked the dark haired, pock-cheeked woman glaring at him through the opening.

"So?"

Titus opened his jacket. "Ms. Bates," he said, lifting the badge clipped to his shirt. "I'm Titus Closson, Town Marshal of Lawrence." He slid his boot forward into the crack of the door. "You worked for Mr. Valentino. You may not know this, but he was murdered a few days ago. Would you answer a few questions for us?"

Her face went ashen and her mouth opened twice before any sound came out. "There is nothing I could or would tell you about Carmine Valentino."

Titus put his hand on the door. "Ms. Bates, you worked for Carmine for more than twenty years. We would really like to talk to you if you could spare us just a few minutes."

The woman's eyes darted nervously between Titus and JoAnna. Her mouth twitched.

"No. It means nothing to me if he was killed." She pushed against the jammed door, looked down. "Look, whoever you are, there is nothing I have to tell. Get your damn foot out of my door and get the fuck out."

"Ms. Bates, please-" JoAnna said, nudging Titus.

"Ma'am this is a murder investigation. If necessary I could make a phone call and get someone with a bigger badge over here. I want you to understand I'm not accusing you of anything, but it's necessary we talk with you."

The woman's eyes shifted to JoAnna. "Who's she?"

JoAnna stepped in front of Titus. "Ms. Bates, I am JoAnna Stanford. I was Carmine Valentino's nurse after you left, until his death. That is really what we would like to talk to you about. Why you left."

Of Mourning Doves and Heroes

The pressure on Titus' foot eased, her eyes scanned him up and down. "You have more identification?"

Titus dug his wallet OUT from his pocket, fingered out a plastic card with his picture and Sheriff Department ID. Then passed it through to the woman. She scrutinized it, comparing the photo. After a moment of hesitation she slipped the chain and opened the door wide enough for them to pass.

The room was simple, a frayed overstuffed recliner, worn sofa and a wicker chair. On the left was a small kitchen with an abused dinette and a short dark hallway at the end. Titus' nose twitched. The place was filled with a faint odor of natural gas. Why do these rooming houses always smell this way?

Behind him Titus heard the woman slip the chain back on the door. "May we sit, Ms. Bates?"

"If you must." She waved her arm toward the sofa.

Titus put the woman in her early forties. She was JoAnna's height, just slightly heavier. Her head was a tangled mass of auburn waves that hung over her ears and neck touching her blue cotton blouse. Her eyes were heavy with dark crescent shadows and her skin pasty with powder that failed to hide the acne scars.

Titus sat on the edge of the sofa. "Ms. Bates, you were with Mr. Valentino for how many years?"

"Twenty-two," she snapped. She turned the wicker chair from the window and faced them. "Get this straight. If Carmine Valentino is dead-" the word caught in her throat, her hand went to her mouth. She turned away and looked down, her shoulders sagging as if burdened. A dozen seconds passed before she turned back and looked Titus in the eye. "I had nothing to do with it."

"Ms. Bates, as I said, we are not charging anyone at this time."

JoAnna put her hand on Titus' arm and leaned forward, "Caroline do you feel alright? It is Caroline isn't it?"

She looked up, nodded. "Yes," she replied.

"Caroline, I worked for Carmine for only four weeks. Given his physical limitations he seemed quite capable and generally a very pleasant man. Did you find him that way?"

"He had his days like everyone does."

"I am sure. Can you recall anyone with whom he might have had a long term problem?"

"No."

Titus settled back into the sofa with his note pad in his hand. "No one? Out of the past, maybe?"

"No."

Of Mourning Doves and Heroes

The room was quiet except for the faint scraping sound of the woman's nervous foot and the creaking of her chair. "Ms. Bates, could you tell us about any visitors he may have had, say within the last two months?"

Her hands worked in her lap. "He never had visitors."

A furrow wrinkled Titus' brow. "Never?"

"The grocery delivery man. The banker occasionally. No one else."

"The banker, Anthony De Gossi?"

Her nod was slight. "Yes."

"How about family?"

"He had family. A brother in New York and another in San Jos—. Listen. Why can't you two just leave me the hell alone? I can't imagine how any of this is going to help anybody."

Titus' mouth twisted. He was getting impatient. "Ms. Bates, please. Answer our questions, then we'll leave. This family, was he in touch with them?"

"No. Christmas cards is all."

"Did you help with the cards? Addresses and all?"

"Sure."

Titus heard a door shut and footsteps on the stairs. He cocked his ear and watched the woman. Her eyes were on the door, her lower lip sucked in, her hands had stopped twisting and the knuckles of her right hand were white from squeezing. The floor squeaked, another door opened and closed. Tension slid from her face, she rubbed the backs of her fingers.

"Ms. Bates, how did Mr. Valentino lose the use of his legs?"

"I wouldn't know."

"In twenty-two years he never mentioned it?"

"Never."

JoAnna cleared her throat. "Excuse me Caroline, may I get a drink?"

"If you must! There's a clean glass on the counter, let it run for a minute."

JoAnna nodded a smile and walked to the kitchen. A moment later she returned with a glass of water. Stepping around Titus' legs she sat and sipped from the glass. "Carmine talked very highly of you, Caroline," she said, holding the glass in both hands.

The woman's gaze dropped to the floor, her hands began working again, a sadness appeared in her eyes and her throat moved as she swallowed.

"How did it happen that you came to work for him, Caroline?"

"I was a nurse."

"But you're not from the Lawrence area, are you?"

"No. Here. Jefferson City. The east side."

Of Mourning Doves and Heroes

Titus looked up from his notes, her foot was still, she seemed to be studying her hands. "It's quite a change for a young girl just out of nursing school to move to a small town like Lawrence," he said.

"That's no big mystery, I was pregnant and unmarried. Even on the east side girls got knocked up."

"So you went away to have the baby," JoAnna said. "A boy I will bet?"

"Yes. Robert." The deep lines around her eyes smoothed, and a smile touched her mouth then vanished as quick as it came.

Titus drummed on his thigh with his fingers. "Ms. Bates, we need to find out if Carmine had any enemies, anyone who would want to see him dead, anyone who would benefit from his death. The sheriff searched the house and was unable to come up with anything like a marriage license, divorce papers, insurance papers. Are you aware of any insurance policy?"

"No!" she shot back.

"Do you have any idea where he would have kept such things?"

She nodded, uncomfortably.

JoAnna slid forward on the edge of the sofa, lifted the glass to her lips for a sip then lowered it carefully to the floor. Her hands came together.

"Caroline was your relationship with Carmine more than nurse-patient?"

The question surprised Titus as well as the woman sitting across the room. Her eyes darted to his then back to JoAnna. He could see something change in the woman's face. Caroline jumped to her feet, spun and strode to the window. She stood to the side and looked out.

JoAnna went to her side and laid her hand on Caroline's shoulder. "I'll listen," she said, softly. After a moment Caroline turned away from the window to JoAnna, her face was blank, then a sob shook her chest and wetness welled into her eyes.

"He's dead." It was a statement meant said to herself. The tears overflowed, she took the tissue JoAnna offered and wiped her cheeks. "He paid enough to have a nice apartment. To raise my son. He put Robert through college. Oh, we crabbed at each other a lot, me and Carmine. He'd get angry, I'd get angry. He even fired me twice."

JoAnna slipped her arm around the woman's shoulders and let her continue. "You asked if we were lovers. There were things we did with each other. Even an old man with no legs can want to touch a woman once in a while." She clamped her mouth shut and turned her stare to Titus. "Is there anything wrong with that?"

"Aaah, no ma'am, there isn't."

Of Mourning Doves and Heroes

Caroline Bates turned away from JoAnna and looked out the window.

Titus followed JoAnna down the steps to the street. The children had the wagon right side up and were struggling to get a yellow dog to sit still long enough for the ride of his life.

"What a strange woman. Did you see the look in her eyes when I told her Valentino was murdered? It wasn't so much surprise as fear."

"Terror would be more like it," JoAnna said.

Titus felt someone watching and wondered if the woman had followed them down the stairs. He unlocked the car door for JoAnna, circled the car, looked back and saw only the two children with the wagon. He turned the key in the lock and slid in. "I have to find a phone," he said, slipping the key in the ignition. The tires squealed as he pulled away from the curb.

"She is scared to death of something, Ty. When I put my hand on her shoulder she was trembling."

"It wasn't us she's afraid of. Those steps on the stairway, did you see the look on her face?

"I don't think she feared that person."

Titus turned his head to look at her, creases lining his forehead.

"I think that was her son, Robert."

His brow curled. "What make's you think that?"

"I can read a face quite well. When she heard the door close she looked like a relieved mother. That and those brogans in the hall. They are young man shoes."

Titus smiled and swung onto Thirty-Eighth. "Very good deduction. Can you read my face that well?"

"Yes."

Feeling a sudden flush of blood he jerked his head and caught a glimpse of her from the corner of his eye. She was looking out the side window, her face turned away from him. "That's scary." He would bet she was smiling.

Three blocks away he spotted a phone booth in front of a convenience store and pulled in. JoAnna crowded into the open doorway watching him feed coins into the slot and dial. A horn blared in the street. The phone rang in his ear, he slipped his arm around her waist and tugged her close. "You were good back there. She wouldn't talk to me. All I got were yes or no answers. You got her to open up," his mouth curled to a grin, he savored the sweet fragrance her close presence brought, then the line clicked.

"Dallas, this is Titus. I just spoke with Carol Bates. Completely uncooperative, to me at least. JoAnna managed to get her to talk some. The woman's scared, Dallas. I mean real scared. And

I'd sure like to know why. Is Captain McKenna still around?"

"Damn! Who else could I talk too? Someone who'll push her a little if it becomes necessary?"

Titus cradled the phone on his shoulder while he dug his note-pad and pen from his pocket then wrote a number and name down. "Thanks, Dallas. And there is something else. The rumor around the schoolyard years ago was that the victim, Valentino, had mob ties at one time and had been injured in the line of duty so to speak. I'd like to find out if there is any thing to it."

"Valentino. Carmine Valentino. 1950's to early 60's I would say."

He looked down at JoAnna, a smile spread across his face, "JoAnna? Well, judging from her performance questioning Carol Bates I'd say she's my new deputy."

Titus gave a quick laugh into the receiver. "I'll have to look it up."

"Thanks, Dallas," he paused, listening. "Yes I will. And thank Leah. Tell her maybe next time."

Titus dropped the receiver on the hook and let go of JoAnna's waist. "Look what up?"

"The definition of deputy," he replied, with a grin as he fumbled through his pockets for another quarter. JoAnna laid a coin on the silver tray. "Thank you." He dropped the coin in the slot and dialed the number on the slip of paper. It rang once and a man's voice came on the line. Titus introduced himself mentioning Dallas Massley's name, filled the party in on some details then asked him for a favor. He paused, listening, then agreed and hung up.

Outside the booth Titus slipped his arm back around JoAnna's waist and led her toward the car conscious of the close warmth of her, the movements against his hip and the brush of her slacks against his leg. He unlocked her door then leaned across the top, his arms spread, fingers splayed looking over the car and gave a tight-lipped sigh. Across the street, three men stood in the doorway of a vacant store. He was quiet for a moment watching the stream of noisy traffic; cars and small trucks mostly, with the occasional motorcycle thrown in all emitting wild beats of notes as though music was the life breath of the machine and the radio the heart.

JoAnna looked puzzled. "What's wrong, Ty?"

"I haven't been in this neighborhood in almost twenty years," he said, his voice soft and melancholy. "It's changed some. The Sea Swing Garment Factory was right there across the street. It went up like a torch on the coldest night of the year, six weeks later that was going up," he waved his finger toward the seedy shops of the strip-mall and the dozen cars parked in the lot. He turned his head and looked beyond the traffic lights down

Of Mourning Doves and Heroes

Stevens Avenue. "Down there a few blocks, where those tenements are, was the flats and the river." Unconsciously he brought his left hand up and rubbed the back of his right shoulder. His gaze slid around to JoAnna. She was quietly looking up at him with her head tilted slightly and her hair sparkling silver in the sunlight.

He turned around to face her and leaned back against the car, "That man on the phone, the first call, was Dallas Massley. My partner for five years. His wife Leah gave me some good advice once." His eyes drifted up, beyond the red lettering over the Quick Shop. "Sandra had been dead for six months and Leah had been caring for Ann Marie on the nights Dallas and I pulled our shift." Titus pointed toward the row of tenements, "Dallas and I were chasing a dealer down a garbage filled alley between a row of plywood shacks when a guy jumped me from behind and stuck a knife in my back. While I was on medical leave recovering, Ann Marie and I spent a lot of evenings with Leah and Dallas. She convinced me to go home to Lawrence and be a parent to Ann Marie. Turned out to be the smartest and best thing I ever did."

He paused, letting his eyes go over JoAnna's face. A cobweb of silver strands stuck to her forehead. She had a small mole at the corner of her mouth and a spatter of freckles high on her cheeks.

Though JoAnna stood perfectly still, he was suddenly aware of her closeness and the absence of the fear it usually brought. He reached for her hands and held them in his and her look turned into a smile that made him smile. I wonder what Leah would say about this he thought, not realizing his lips were moving.

"What?" she asked softly.

"I was just wondering what Leah would say about us."

A devilish twinkle danced in her eyes and white teeth flashed. "She would give you the second best piece of advice of your life."

Titus threw his head back and laughed. "And that would be?"

"That life in this time is finite. Don't go on to the next one with regrets," she answered with a wicked grin.

He looked down at her hands, warm in his and made up his mind. "Let's get a bite. Chinese?"

"I'm famished," she replied.

-9-

Ablock before the intersection of Fairview and Vista their conversation faded to silence making the squawk of the police radio seem louder. The yellow glow of the street light lit the car briefly as Titus made the turn and he stole a glance in her direction. Joanna's silhouette hadn't changed in forty years, the angular cut of her face, the rise of her breasts and her thin waist. The rock in the pit of his stomach rose and fell with each breath. He wondered if she was as nervous as he was. He chuckled to himself remembering the way the chopsticks had shook in his fingers when she'd asked him to spend the night. He'd had to finish his Lomain with a fork.

The trembling came back as he slowed the car at the curb and stopped in the circle of pale illumination from the street lamp. Her face caught the light as she rummaged through her purse and produced her keys. Her eyes were wide and the lower lip she had sucked between her teeth came loose, opening into a smile. She released a sigh. "Are you as nervous as I am?" she asked.

He twisted uncomfortably in his seat trying to gain room in his slacks. "That's not my trouble at the moment," he answered, straining to lighten his voice. "My problem is I'm too embarrassed to get out of the car."

Her bright eyes moved over him and stopped on his face. He felt her smile and reached through the dark letting his fingers find the back of her hand. Speaking softly in a voice that carried the air of wonder. "It's a wonderful problem that I haven't had in years," he said letting his touch linger.

He jerked his hand back and shook his head violently wishing for a few seconds of thoughts of blue sky and white clouds.

Titus stood outside the car for a long minute looking into the dark night, calming himself then hurried up the walk to the steps where JoAnna waited.

Hanging their coats JoAnna closed the closet door and turned to him. Catching her hand he drew her to him and slipped one hand around her waist, his other hand went to her chin and lifted it until their gaze met. He could smell the lavender of her. It seemed to excite and calm him at the same time. Their lips touched briefly and he drew back until he could see her face, marveling at the passion surging through him. He caressed her cheek. Her hand went to his, moved it to her waist then slid up his back as she pressed into his arms. They kissed again, gently at first, then her lips parted and he tasted her mouth. Instantly his pulse soared as they learned the other's mouth. His hands slid across her back and down over her round bottom. And when he lifted, drawing her against him, a muted groan came from somewhere deep within her. He felt her arms relax and heard a low moan. Then he felt a thudding against his chest. Not sure if it was from him or her. Then her hand slid between them and over his chest. She pushed back, both gulping ragged breaths. After a moment the pounding slowed and he heard himself say her name. Lifting his hand to her lips she gently kissed his fingers, then led him to the bedroom.

*   *   *

She came to him in a blue satin nightgown and slid into the bed beside him. They rolled into each other's arms and the years sprang through the clouds leaving behind two eager, panting lovers.

"Do you remember the first time, Ty?" Her look was gentle and loving. The radiator in the corner clicked like a grandfather clock counting the minutes till sunrise. They lay facing each other, the covers kicked in a pile off the foot of the bed. Through the screened window the Indian Summer sunrise cast in firings of brilliant molten red steel and poured into the room. JoAnna raised up on her left elbow and looked down with her eyes as rich as French chocolate. Her lips parted and stretched to a smile and her fingers lightly teased the silver hairs on his chest as she awaited his answer.

Titus opened his eyes, sliding one hand behind his head. With the other he caressed her arm. "Yes, I remember. I remember all three times." He let seconds pass. His mind focused on the soft, silky feel of her skin under his fingertips as he moved his hand along her arm to her shoulder and down her breast. He turned his head into her breasts and inhaled. She smelled like sweet cream.

"It seems an awful long time ago," he said, letting the words run down. A pause, the dust of years settled and coated them with memories.

"We were so young." she said, finally. "You were the first, you know."

He looked up. "And you were mine."

His eyes caught the curl at the corners of her mouth. "It was that obvious?" he asked.

She chuckled and her smile expanded, creasing her cheeks. "You've improved with age, and experience," she said, leaning forward. Her hand went to his face as she set a kiss on his lips, his cheek, the bridge of his nose and then pulled back.

Of Mourning Doves and Heroes

He felt her gaze exploring, taking him all in and strangely it didn't make him uncomfortable.

He cradled her breast gently, feeling its delicacy in his palm, then gently rolled the nipple in his fingers feeling it go from soft to hard in his fingertips. "Experience improves us all."

"Not necessarily, love. Sex tells a lot about a person. How you feel about yourself, how you feel about others. It's a gauge of a person's sensitivity, but more importantly, their self-confidence. You are a sensitive and confident person, Ty."

He blushed remembering how they had enjoyed each other through the night. "And you sure do wonders for my self-confidence."

Through the window the brilliant sunrise was softening to an orange glow. She sat up, doubling her legs back, and looked down at him. "So, I please you then?"

He raised himself onto his elbow and propped his head in his hand. "Please me?" His gaze moved over her, a grin tugged at his lips. "Just the sight of you pleases me, Jo."

She still had a pleasant figure. Though the years had taken a toll on her breasts, her legs were surprisingly firm and shapely, her waist thin, and the patch of light chestnut hair where her thighs came together made her look young and vital. He remembered the brush of it on his cheek, and her taste; a shudder slipped through him. "You are as beautiful and exciting, as I remember."

"I hoped you would think so."

He caressed the arch of her foot letting his eyes flow over her, astonished at the desire she could arouse in him. His hand feathered along her leg, his fingers caressing the firm muscles of her thigh. She shifted, letting his hand fall to the soft inside of her right leg, then leaned back on her hands exposing more of herself.

The Mound of Venus, Titus thought, that's what the Romans called it. Elegant. He touched the soft folds and opened her, his fingers finding her wetness. He heard her breath catch and looked at her face. Her eyes were closed, a distant warm look had settled over her face. "Ummmmmm."

"And just as bold," he added.

Her eyes came open. "I want you again."

Titus felt the beginnings of arousal. "That just might be possible."

With a wonderfully wicked look on her face, she brushed his hand away, gently pushed him onto his back. Then she bent her head and drew his penis between her lips and in a moment he felt himself alive again.

-10-

The sun had popped over the tops of the trees and begun evaporating the feathery frosty glaze that had settled over everything in the valley. Titus burst through the green door of the cafe and crossed the street, swatting the rolled morning paper against his leg with every stride. He took the steps of the Grand Hotel two at a time and pushed through the door. Inside he surveyed the clinking, crowded dining room then located the table he wanted. Madelyn Fisher, alone at a nearby table, wished him a good morning. A young woman in a green apron started toward him with a menu then stopped when she saw the set of his face. Titus' lips barely moved, "Not this morning, Sally."

The clinking faded as faces looked up including the three in the corner booth. He took a deep breath, letting his chest fall slowly and banged the paper against his thigh one more time. Then moved with ease around the tables to the booth and looked down at the three men; Tony De Gossi, Jamie Bender, and a red bearded, balding man Titus didn't know.

Tony De Gossi carefully set the partially eaten doughnut onto the plate, picked up a paper napkin, planted his elbows on the table and wiped his fingers. "Something I can do for you, Closson?" he asked, balling the napkin between his palms.

The rolled newspaper Titus held clenched in his fist waved slowly in the air. He looked down into the boyish face then around the table at the other two. The morning paper lay open on the table and folded to the interview. The clinking in the room all but stopped and the murmur of conversation ceased.

"May I sit, Mr. De Gossi?" Titus asked, his voice held under control by the tight muscles in his throat.

"Sure, Closson. Come to concede the election?"

Jamie Bender snickered then quickly sobered under Titus' stare, which had dropped to the red headed man.

"Marshal, this is Leonard Barnes," Tony said, indicating the red haired man.

Titus recognized the name. 'Lenny Barnes', Attorney. With a penchant for taking clients on the edge of the law.

Of Mourning Doves and Heroes

Barnes, coffee cup dangling on his fingers, slid across the seat leaving his grease covered dishes. Titus lowered himself onto the edge of the seat, swept the dishes aside and leaned over the table. He slapped the morning paper twice with his left hand, then jabbed the rolled paper at De Gossi. His voice was low. "This is bullshit and libelous and you know it."

De Gossi grinned. His tone mocking, his voice rising and falling as he spoke. "Now Closson, you know as well as I do in a political campaign libel doesn't count. Don't get so serious. You'll still be on the public dole after the elections. Your pal Sheriff Watkins will put you on as a process server or something. It'll be an easy way to end a nothing career."

The muscles across Titus' back bunched and a tic throbbed at his right temple. From the corner of his eye he saw a grin on Jamie Bender's face.

Titus inhaled deeply then let the rage seep out slowly until his trembling hand steadied. "You know Tony, you don't give the people of this town enough credit. I was thinking seriously about dropping out of the race, letting you have this nothing job. But, in this article you insulted my intelligence and that of the citizens of Lawrence. Valentino was murdered, Tony. The county crime lab confirmed that much. So it looks to me like you were either totally uninformed; or just making foolish statements or deliberately misleading." He paused, fighting to keep his breath even. His stare burrowed into the white toothed face of Tony De Gossi across the table, beside him he felt Leonard Burnes shift in his seat. "And as for any questionable activities going on around here, maybe you're right. Maybe I should start asking questions. Maybe I should start at the Sun Dancer."

De Gossi wet his lips.

Titus felt a hand on his arm. "Marshal," Lenny Barnes said, "Mr. De Gossi has nothing to do with the Sun Dancer, and besides it's outside the town limits so it's of no concern of yours."

Titus stared at the hand on his arm, then at Lenny. The man had a pasted on lawyer's smile across his face.

Titus' eyes hardened. "Yes it is, Mr. Barnes," Titus replied, laying his right hand across the lawyer's hand. His squeeze tightened around the man's wrist with each word he spoke. "But as I'm sure you know any peace officer in the county is also a sworn deputy." By the time Titus got to the word Deputy, Lenny Barnes had tears in his eyes.

-11-

The new moon, brilliant neon in the clear black sky, cast surreal shadows through the tiny hamlet of Goodview. Ann Marie checked her mirror, slowed and turned left at the church onto the narrow county road that would get her home a few minutes faster. As the last dark house slipped by she studied the mirror, curious that the headlights behind her had also turned.

The road narrowed and the tires thumped across the rough-surface bridge over a shallow creek. On the right two red specks appeared in the dark grassy ditch then vanished in a blink. She lifted her foot, prepared to stop, not wanting to hit an animal or have an accident this late at night on a deserted stretch of road.

After a moment she relaxed and played back through her mind what she had learned from her reporter friend Todd Peabody this evening in the coffee shop. And what Sergeant Shinder, the booking officer from the Jefferson City jail had told them. Tony De Gossi and Monty Hammer had been arrested October eighteenth, nineteen eighty-eight at one thirty AM outside the Clover Leaf Bar. Each had a small amount of marijuana on them. And each had made a long distance phone call after being booked. Around eight AM orders had came to release the two. According to the Sergeant, the call came from the shift supervisor, a Lieutenant Carl Rosen. When Todd explained he had asked Lieutenant Rosen about the incident and the lieutenant claimed he couldn't remember, Sergeant Shinder had rolled his eyes.

Ann Marie shifted her attention from the narrow macadam road sliding under her lights to the mirror. The headlights were far back, but still there. A yellow sign glared for an instant. Her toe found the high beams. The dark hulk of the Diamond Corners Feed Store slid by in the night. On a terraced hillside on the left a floodlight lit a farmhouse and barn.

Why would someone intervene with the police for Tony De Gossi? Without the intervention the charges would probably have been reduced to disorderly conduct anyway.

The road ahead was straight for a few miles, she knew. Her eyes flicked to the mirror. Pressing down on the accelerator she was relieved to watch the lights behind fade to yellow dots.

After the sergeant left she had sat and talked with Todd. It seemed being a banker's son had not helped Tony De Gossi at the academy, as he had ranked twenty-first in a class of thirty before being booted out. She remembered Tony as he had been in high school; strutting, always the big shot. Why would anyone intercede on his behalf? She thought over Todd's answer. The Mob. The rumor on the streets in the seamy parts of Jefferson City was that the Sun Dancer, a roadhouse with a history of mob-connected owners two miles north of Lawrence, had been sold off to someone from Sweet Springs.

She toyed with her hair. Was it possible, as Todd had claimed, that Tony De Gossi had developed a connection with the mob? And what would he do with the Sun Dancer? As far as she knew, it had always been run as a legitimate business. She had danced to the country/rock bands on Friday and Saturday nights since she was old enough to get through the door.

She turned the radio up a notch. With friends in the county clerk's office it wouldn't be too hard to find out who really did buy the Sun Dancer.

The road turned left, dropped over a long hill then straightened to Mill Creek. Fifteen minutes from home, she thought.

Suddenly lights glared bright in the mirror. She felt her pulse jump. The vehicle had come up too fast. Someone was following!

She gripped the wheel with both hands as fear grew in her stomach and clawed its way into her throat. The lights slipped to the left, then came up in the sideview mirror. Who? Her foot stiffened on the accelerator, the needle pushed past sixty. The bridge was just ahead. This was crazy!

The beams stayed steady. Who could it be? A cold chill that started at the back of her neck sent prickles down her arms. If someone knows it's me then they know where I've been!

Her eyes flicked back and forth from the road to the bright glare in the sideview mirror. The fool's going to pass!

From the corner of her eye she saw the yellow pennant sign flash by and lifted her foot from the accelerator. The vehicle slipped a half-length ahead. What the hell!!??

The beams of headlights picked out the white diagonal markings on the bridge abutment. She jammed the brakes. Her scream fused with the raucous thunder of ripping metal.

*   *   *

The ringing phone on the bedside table jarred Titus from deep slumber into a sitting position, staring frantically around the pitch-black room for the source of the horrible noise.

He fumbled for the light and lifted the receiver. "Yahaaa," he said through the cotton of his dry mouth.

"Marshal Closson?" said a female voice.

"Yes?"

"This is the sheriff's office. There is a five eighteen on county road 65 at the Mill Creek Bridge. The deputy on the scene says to inform you the driver is Ann Marie Closson. A Medic unit has been dispatched, Sir."

The phone fell away from his ear. "Sir? Sir?" the voice repeated.

Titus swallowed hard to open his throat. "Aha, Thanks. I'm on my way."

The night was giving it up to whiskers of gray in the east when Titus slowed at the county road 65 turnoff, the dome light flickering red like devil's eyes in the windows of Jack & Jill's towing. He made the turn onto the narrow blacktop and pressed the accelerator down.

It was a fear-chilled ten-mile drive to the Mill Creek Bridge during which Titus, dread roosting deep in his heart, would sort through a lifetime of memories. Sandra's gaunt face and sunken eyes filled with the terrible pain she could no longer hide, or bear. So weak from her losing battle with the cancer that she could no longer speak. And the skinny dark-haired, dark-eyed girl sitting bravely on the edge of the bed gently patting her mother's hand, sure that if she proved strong enough and prayed hard enough her mother would beat the disease that ate at her. He recalled the years filled with nights of quiet talk of the things and ways of the world. Hours of reading together, nights of carrying a little sleeping girl from the sofa to her bed, tucking the covers around her neck and brushing strings of black hair from her forehead to kiss her goodnight. He remembered the hundreds of times he had stood in the pitch blackness of the night looking down to where she slept quietly, listening to her faint breathing. His own breaths falling in with her rhythm. And the feeling he loved so much, a feeling of wholeness that had always filled him, a feeling of worth only the unconditional love his daughter could provide.

He had learned to live without the companionship of a mate, could he---. He shuddered and gripped the wheel. "Please be okay, Sunshine." He cried the words out in the darkness of the car, then as if wishing would make it so, he repeated his words over and over and over as the narrow black tar road slid under his headlights.

His heart was rolling in his chest then nearly burst through his throat at the sudden blaze of approaching red and white strobes. He eased off the accelerator and pulled to the shoulder of the road letting the screaming ambulance pass. A trembling, terrifying moan escaped his throat and a shudder shook him to his boots leaving him faint. With pounding heart he stared at the mirror until the flashing lights dropped over a hill.

Find out what happened, roared through his brain. His foot hit the accelerator, tires pounded the underside of the car with dirt and screeched as they bit into asphalt. Before he reached the top of the hill he slid to a stop on the shoulder, cut the wheels and in a spray of gravel swung the car around. "To hell with what happened," he shouted. Minutes later he was closing in on the ambulance.

Titus swung onto the horseshoe drive and stopped short of the canopy and the ambulance parked under it. He sprung from the car then froze. His dome light pulsed a red fire across his face as he stood beside the car with his hands clasping the open door and watching a half dozen white clothed figures rush through the yellow lit doorway. He was afraid his legs would give way if he moved.

He watched one of the white cloaked shapes open the rear doors of the ambulance. Watched the gurney come out to waiting hands, watched the wheels drop and watched the cluster of white figures rush the glass doors. He heard the doors hiss as they parted then watched them slide shut. Ann Marie was gone.

*   *   *

The rays of the rising sun felt warm on the back of Titus' neck as he walked along the edge of the road, his hands jammed deep in his jacket pockets. Behind him JoAnna stopped, picked a sliver of red plastic lens from the frozen crust of earth, examined it then tossed it away. He was glad he had asked her to ride along.

A dozen yards from the car where a steel culvert passed under the roadway; he stopped and looked out over acres of tall brown marsh grass. Around the distant edge of the expansive field of dry grass a Tamarack forest stood in a blaze of brilliant orange. At his feet tiny stars of ice crystals had formed in the freshly scored earth.

Moving deliberately he followed the agonizing scar down to the sole, twisted and scrapped scrub oak. In the trampled soil the sun's rays caught the chrome headlight ring from Ann Marie's car. He picked it up, turned it in his gloved hands. Ann Marie had insisted and he hadn't listened. The muscles across the back of his shoulders knotted. If he could find out who was responsible for this, he'd twist the thing around the bastard's throat. He looked up at JoAnna who was watching him from the edge of the road, now wishing she wasn't here. If he were alone he would be free to rail against the son-of-a-bitch who did this to his daughter. If he were alone he would scream.

Of Mourning Doves and Heroes

He gave in to his need for another breath and looked down at the shiny metal ring in his hand. A crease of red seeped from the base of his thumb. The sharp-edged piece of scrap had sliced his hand. "Shit," he spat, letting anger spill.

Ross Tarry

-12-

His face set in a grim scowl as he picked up his tools and stood studying the temporary ramp over the threshold of the back door. That will work for a few days, Titus thought. I'll get someone to make the permanent changes.

He recalled Carmine Valentino's house; hard floors, wide doors with no sills, the bathroom with the lift in the shower. He bit down on his lip until the pain forced the torturous thoughts away. She would walk again. The doctors claimed her right leg was already stronger than the left. He knew her determination would push her once the depression eased. He looked around at the clock. Nearly ten. He had told her he would be there to get her by noon. He would never have dreamed how much he had missed her over the past months.

The wherrrrp of a power tool came from down the hall, a young man in gray coveralls stood in the front doorway. "Almost done Mr. Closson. Maybe another ten minutes. Rusty's sinking the anchors now."

"Good, Terry." Titus set the tools on the corner of the counter and followed the man back down the hall. Standing in the doorway, Titus felt his whole body tighten. The muscles in the back of his shoulders bunched up into knots as he looked over the array of aluminum pipes and bars over Ann Marie's bed. It was similar to the one in the rehabilitation center but without the weights and pulleys that were used to build up the movement and strength in her legs. A feeling, like a cold breeze, started at the back of his neck. Anthony De Gossi, if I can prove you did this to her, you will pray to be left in this good of shape.

The thin balding man on his knees with the drill at the foot of Ann Marie's bed stopped his work and looked up. "Hope this works out for Ms. Closson, Marshal."

He wasn't the marshal any more, but had discovered many of the towns' people still referred to him as such. Once a Colonel always a Colonel.

"She's a tough young woman, Rusty. She'll make it." Every time he'd said those words over the last two months his mouth had gone dry. Fate can step into a life and change it in an instant.

The young man brushed past Titus and stopped in the doorway. "We had to strengthen the floor from underneath, but it's going to be nice and solid."

"Thanks, Terry."

When the men left he carried his tools through the dusting of late spring snow to the garage and headed into Sweet Springs.

Ann Marie was in the kitchen when he came back. Her hair was tossed from sleep, her thin legs resting on the steel pads of the wheelchair.

She had water heating on the front burner of the stove and bread in the toaster on the table. "Good morning," Titus said, in the most cheerful voice he could muster.

Without looking at him she pushed the wheels sending her chair across the kitchen to the refrigerator. "It's morning all right," she replied, jerking the door open.

Titus watched, his face bristling. Over the last months he had checked every car in town for some sign. A scratch, an unexplained dent. Fighting the urge to kick something, he watched Ann Marie jockey the chair around until she could reach the butter and jam. She dropped the containers in her lap and slammed the door shut.

The muscles in his face hurt as he crossed the room to the sink. He got a cup and silverware from the drainer and set a place at the table. He was so thankful she hadn't been killed. Yet it was killing him to see her like this, filled with so much pain, anger. The anger he could deal with. He shared it. It was the pain he saw in her eyes and the growing frustration on her face at the difficulty in doing the simplest things that ate at his heart. ACCEPTING HER NEW CHALLENGE, that wimpy counselor at the Rehab Center called it. SHE WOULD IN TIME, the man had said. ANGER BUILDS THE WILL TO FIGHT, he said. It nearly did. She almost came out of the wheelchair at him.

Well so far he hadn't seen much progress.

"If you go out to feed the doves, wear a jacket. It doesn't look like we'll see the sun today."

She spun around. "Where are you going?"

"To Sweet Springs. To see Ray Watkins."

She eyed him sharply. "You're going to take the job, then?"

"Yes," he responded, meeting her stare for a moment before turning away.

*   *   *

Linda was on the phone. She looked up, held the receiver away and said, "Sheriff Watkins is expecting you Ty. Give me a second and I'll tell him you're here."

Titus leaned against the high counter. He probably could have won his job back if he had stayed in the race. But in one way the accident had stolen something from him also. He had little stomach to go through a public battle. Another thing, Ann Marie needed him. Just as she did when Sandra died. He would never forget the look on her face when he told her it was her legs. It had gone from startled comprehension, to paste, to red with fury in seconds.

The morning paper caught his eye. He turned it to read the headlines: SWEET SPRINGS MAN CHARGED IN DEATH OF FOUR-YEAR OLD BOY

He didn't feel like reading further and shoved it away.

"The same child that "fell" from the second story balcony last fall, remember?" Helen cradled the phone. "Looks like the system failed again."

Ray Watkins, his red hair blazing in the noon sun pouring through the blinds, settled back in his leather trimmed oak chair and looked up at Titus. Behind him on the top of a matching bookcase weighted with gilt-edged volumes, tiny red dots blinked in sequence across the front of the scanner, the faint decibels of squeaks and crackles barely discernable.

Titus was somber. He turned the thin leather wallet over and over in his hands before he opened it. Inside was a white and blue plastic card identifying Titus V. Closson as Special Investigator, Bergess County Sheriff Department.

Titus' mouth pursed in a frown. Despite what Ann Marie said, this was a good move. Salary, benefits and a county pension if he stayed until he was sixty-five. And what better position to check into Ann Marie's accident that was no accident.

Titus flipped the wallet closed and slid it into his inside jacket pocket. "What's my first assignment, Ray?"

"For now you stick with the Valentino case." Ray Watkins brushed his hands across his desk. "What's the word on how Ann Marie's last surgery turned out?"

Titus scrunched his mouth, shook his head. "With so much damage to the left femur there wasn't much surface to reattach muscle. The biggest problem is the nerve stem in her right leg. She may never regain its use. And the left will never be very strong. The doctors keep saying she will walk again, but I get the feeling they aren't as hopeful as they once were."

Ray leaned forward, looking down thoughtfully at his desk a moment before looking up. "Shows how primitive medical science really is. We expect to be fixed, replace the broken part with one that works. It doesn't always happen. Ann Marie's got moxy. That will do more for her than anything."

"I know. I just wish she'd have gotten a look at the car. Something."

Of Mourning Doves and Heroes

Ray held up a thin folder. "The official report on Tony De Gossi's problem with the State Patrol Academy. Not much in it but enough to get him booted."

He handed the report across the desk. Titus took the document, pulled a chair to the corner of the desk, and sat.

"Got caught with his pants down, so to speak," Ray grinned.

Titus read through the report. Tony De Gossi and another cadet, Monty Hammer were caught in a john sweep in Jefferson's tenderloin. A body search at the scene turned up a small amount of marijuana. The two were held overnight pending charges then released the next day with no charges made. The following day the academy commander, J.J.Dearwood dismissed the two: "Without Particulars".

Titus tossed the folder on the desk. "Without Particulars?"

"That's a bit unusual, according to the source."

Titus picked up the report again. "Interesting. Can I keep this?"

"It's your copy. Actually it's Ann Marie's."

Titus' mouth twisted. He pushed himself out of the leather chair; walked to the window and let the sun's rays warm his face. He looked out on Main Street through the thick glass and bars to the activity of the street. The sun was a shill in its brightness and the sky a cloudless charlatan blue. The Hawk, as the Indians called it, was blowing from the north. Leggy women and white shirted men hurrying to lunch, hunched their shoulders against the first real chill of late fall. "How much was the small amount? Wasn't it weighed?"

"No one seemed to know anything about it at the city attorney's office."

Titus twisted his head around and looked back at the redheaded sheriff. "Ann Marie thinks someone intervened."

"I would say so but who could have shown enough interest in Tony De Gossi to put a word in for the man? According to the report there wasn't enough marijuana to bring a felony count against him. And the john thing, he would have walked with a lecture, not much more. It's the rich guy's kid thing, Ty. Only Tony De Gossi isn't a kid."

"No, but he's doing okay since becoming the Marshal. He's bought a big, shiny four-wheel drive truck with lots of chrome, and talked the town board into leasing it from him."

"Shrewd."

"No, crooked. He may not have been in the car, but I would bet my life he knew about it. Ann Marie was learning things that could have been a problem for him. Granted, this incident at the police academy was minor but the marshal job was important for some reason. Probably to cover his plans for the Sun Dancer. In two months he's turned it into the hot spot in the county."

Titus heard the sheriff's sigh. "Yaah. I guess I'm going to have to pay him a visit soon. Welcome him to this side of the law."

Titus rubbed two fingers back and forth across his forehead. "I wonder about that, Ray."

Outside on the sidewalk, ignored by the noontime bustle, two young males in torn jeans, leather jackets and headbands approached. They glanced sideways up at the gray granite of the court house then darted into the street through a blare of horns to the other side.

Titus glanced down at the report in his hand. "What about this Monty Hammer?"

"Nothing. A farm boy from out state."

"Where?

"Spinks Corners. Near Hargrove."

Titus slid the folder in his fingers. "I may look him up."

Ray's chair creaked as he turned back to his desk. "Tell Ann Marie that's all I could come up with and I have nothing about the big sedan she thinks ran her off the road."

Titus turned from the window and put his hands on the back of the chair. "Thanks, Ray. Enough of this. Come up with anything on Valentino's computer or the discs?"

"Nothing that would relate to his murder. The guy was really into games and flowers. A botanist would love to get a hold of some of that stuff. Charts, graphs, essays. Very detailed. Catalogued and cross-catalogued. He must have kept track of every flower he had ever grown for twenty years. Everything you could imagine. Each year was plotted, what was planted where. Followed by pages of things like planting conditions, weather conditions, fertilizer, insects, disease. And pages and pages of summary. I'll tell you Ty, there is an awful lot there. If no one turns up to claim it, maybe I'll turn the plant records over to the university."

"Nothing of a personal nature?" Titus said, settling back into the leather chair.

"No. Why?" Ray asked, intrigued.

"I just find it strange that no personal records were found such as insurance policies, divorce papers. Those kinds of things."

Ray sat forward folding his arms across the desk and started to speak, but Titus went on. "I know. Too some people---," he stopped in mid-sentence to realign his thoughts, then continued. "Take me for example. All my IMPORTANT PAPERS are in a box somewhere in the garage, but they're around. This Valentino had lists telling where lists were. It doesn't figure."

Of Mourning Doves and Heroes

Ray brought his hands up, laced his fingers together and rested his chin. "I see what you're saying."

Titus stared thoughtfully through the window. "His nurse, Caroline Bates said he was at his computer all the time. Sometimes late into the night. He had wide, varied interests. I just find it hard to believe he was playing games all that time." Titus stopped short. "A magazine. Writer's Digest." When he turned back he was caught by the sheriff's stare. "There was a magazine for writers on his desk. I think he was a writer."

"A book?"

"Maybe. Maybe his memoirs."

"Well the last twenty-five years weren't much."

"No, but if there is any truth to these old rumors about him being in with the mob at one time, his memoirs might prove interesting."

Ray Watkins lifted his chin from his clasped hands, his mouth pursed. "That might prove to be the motive for his murder."

The black box beside the telephone dinged and the sheriff pressed the button. "Yes, Linda."

The woman's voice coming through the speaker was crisp and professional. "Sheriff, Lawrence Fire Department is responding to a ten-twenty-two at the address of that homicide you and Marshal Closson are working on."

Titus jerked up stunned, his eyes wide. For a long second the two men stared at each other, then Titus was on his feet. The sheriff leaned forward and touched the button on the box. "Helen, get the sector unit over there if it's available, and have the deputy call me." He swung his chair halfway around, turned up the volume of the scanner and leaned back. "Just as I was thinking we ought to have another look." When the sheriff turned around Titus' back was going through the door.

*   *   *

It was a little after three o'clock when Titus walked into ROXIE'S TAVERN. Parts of Jefferson City had changed drastically in the twenty years he'd been away. Even ROXIE'S. The big, slow ceiling fans were gone and dark sturdy tables had replaced the booths. The heavy blend of beer and frying oil; the stack of bottles behind the bar were as familiar as the two black-haired, gold chained middle-aged men in blazers sitting at the back table. They were pouring over folded racing forms and the three young James Dean look alikes at the end of the bar. Not the faces, he was too far beyond them in age, but the familiar memory, drawn from the past like a curled photo pulled reluctantly from a dusty shoebox. He half expected, if he were to turn to the door, to see a cocky young uniformed Titus V. Closson come strutting through.

The talk stopped and they all looked up as he approached the bar including the thin, hollow-cheeked gray-headed man bent over washing glasses. Titus unzipped his jacket, swung his leg over the corner stool next to the waitress station and ordered a burger and a beer.

The bartender set up a bottle and a glass then moved to the end of the bar to the grill. He came back wiping his hands on his apron. "Name's Reno. Ain't seen you before."

Titus pulled a twenty from his shirt pocket, slid it across the bar and tipped the bottle, half filling the small glass. "Would have if you'd been around thirty years ago."

Reno smiled showing teeth chipped and spotted with silver. "Was around. Just not here."

Reno was eager to talk and Titus had finished his sandwich and was into his second beer when he looked around. "The phone still back by the can?"

Reno nodded, glanced at the two in the corner and pointed with his thumb. "It's free," he said.

The two horseplayers at the table briefly looked up as Titus walked by then went back to handicapping the next race. Memories rushed back. Memories of white haired men with the strong, black, twisted cigars that thirty years before had sat in booths in the same exact spot.

Titus had lifted his finger, allowing the phone one more ring before hanging up when a click and Dallas Massley's voice came on the line. "Dallas. It's Titus."

From the corner of his eye he saw one of the men from the table step into the hall, see the phone was busy and stop. "Well I could lie to you and say she's coming along fine, but I won't. Listen, there's a guy here waiting to call his grandmother, so I better hurry. I'm at a joint named ROXIE'S. Remember it?"

"I'm on my way to see old Flori."

"I will. Anything on De Gossi?"

The man in the sport jacket looked nervously at his watch. "Thanks. Let me know. And another thing. Lenny Barnes seems to have found a new client. He might be De Gossi's mob connection."

Titus slid back onto his stool, hooked his heels on the bottom rung and poured his glass full. Down the bar Reno opened three beers, set them in front of the three jocks and moved back to Titus' end wiping his hands on a bar towel.

"Ever hear of a guy named Angelo Flori?" Titus asked.

"Yeah. Still lives over the drug store on the corner."

"Does he come around much?"

"Once or twice a week. If he can get out. Legs bother him bad. Stops in on his way back from the grocer for a shot of the old licorice." Reno paused twisting the towel into a rope and looked Titus over. "So you know old Flori, Huh."

"Ought to," Titus replied. "Back then he run this place for the Syndicate. Who runs it now?"

Reno's face changed, his eyes darted around. He wet his lips and leaned close. "Who are you, Mister?"

Titus let his smile come slow. He lifted his drink. "An old friend of Angelos. Name's Titus Closson," he added, over the top of his glass.

Titus could feel by the way Reno's eyes searched his face the old bartender was reviewing their conversation for something he maybe shouldn't have said. Evidently satisfied for the moment, Reno nodded once and moved down the bar to wait on a new customer.

Titus drained the glass and turned on the stool. Shutting out the increased banter of the three young men, he looked out through the window, beyond the colored twists of neon tubes to the building across the street. The thick black letters on the marquee of what he remembered as the State Theater now advertised the lowest furniture prices in the city. THE GODFATHER now spells no money down.

The movie every payday had been a ritual for the newlyweds. Beginning as a commitment of time he had made to Sandra when she agreed to the move to Jefferson and his joining the police force. A commitment he had tried to keep, even when cash was short. A movie, a burger and the three block walk back to the apartment holding hands and talking. A commitment he soon learned also had meaning for him. For Sandra, their time together was a sign she wasn't being taken for granted. A time when their togetherness eased the eternal fears of being a cop's wife. A time when she laughed and tossed her thick black hair in the sultry August air. A time that triggered their passion. It was, he was sure, on one of those evenings when Ann Marie was conceived. Then cancer came and his life was never to be the same.

A red and white paramedic unit screamed by the window and faded down the street. Titus heard his name and jerked around. Reno had his hand on the empty bottle.

"Might as well," Titus said, looking at his watch. "Still got some time."

Reno set up another bottle, brought back the change. "What brings you back to the neighborhood? Slumming?"

Titus tipped the bottle and poured half a glass. "Old times, I guess."

The door opened and two young women dressed to the nines in tight skirts, fake jewelry and heels came in. Reno greeted each by name, then in a lowered voice said, "These two sing at the Clover Club down the street."

Titus turned his head and watched the two women take a table along the wall. When he turned back, Reno had set a tray on the bar and was filling two ice-jammed glasses with gin.

"The neighborhood changed much since you hung around?" he asked.

Titus' eyes drifted down the bar to the young hoods, then to the two players in the corner. "The buildings look older and the people look younger, is all."

"Hear yah," Reno replied, twisting a bit of lime into each glass.

Titus looked around at the two women. One, digging through a small black leather bag, came out with a pack of cigarettes.

"Those two interest you?"

Titus turned back slowly. "No. Just wondering. Out kind of early in the day aren't they?"

"Happy hour you know," Reno said, looking around at the clock. He picked the tray off the bar, his mouth screwed into a twist of disdain. "Be busier and noisier then hell for 'while, then things will quiet some 'fore the real riffraff comes in."

Titus picked up his glass and the open bottle and moved to a table where he could watch the door. The two horseplayers were still making their trips to the phone. A red haired woman in tight slacks came on duty to wait tables. The gloss burgundy of her lips and the rose highlights on her flat cheeks were designed to draw attention away from the creases under her eyes, but her hands gave her away.

Titus poured the glass full, lifted it, and solemnly watched the rising effervescence. Where does the desire to return to the past come from? We can't change what's gone, what's done. The memories, even if they are not all pleasant, always seem comfortable, but the actual coming back is never the same. It only contaminates those memories.

Enough of this. He shoved the chair back and caught Reno's eye. Then carried the glass and the empty bottle to the bar, laid a five dollar bill against the back rail and stepped out into the gray, chilly afternoon. At the corner he stopped at the liquor store; then paper bag in his hand took the elevator to the second floor.

Titus hadn't thought of Angelo Flori until Dallas mentioned that if anyone would remember the Carmine Valentino story it would be Angelo. Thirty years ago Angelo Flori was the *padrone* of the River Bluff neighborhood, the patriarch. The man with connections to the men with connections. Aging had not been easy on the man, shrinking him down to bones, turning his hair to fine wisps of white cobwebs, creasing the paper thin skin around his eyes so that it hung in tiny folds and stealing the timbre that Titus remembered from his voice. But time seemed to have neglected to inform him of his diminished personage, saying nothing when Titus introduced himself until after the presentation of the gift.

With a faint tip of the head Angelo Flori leaned his cane against the doorjamb and took the brown bag from Titus.

"Sure, I remember you." He tucked the bag under his left arm then extended his shaky hand. "You said you wanted to talk about the old days. Don't know if I can help."

Titus closed the door behind him and followed the aged man into a comfortable flat that was too warm and smelled of oil and onion. "You can help. Dallas reminded me that nothing ever happened around here you didn't know about."

"You see I have lived to be an old man." Leaning heavily on a cane the aging Don set two glasses on the table then lowered his gaunt body into the straight-backed armchair at the head of the table. He propped the cane against the edge and with a shaky hand, twisted the cover from the bottle of anisette.

"Sit," he said, indicating the chair facing him. "Dallas used to talk about you." The bottle clinked against the rim as he poured two fingers of the clear liquid into each glass. He pushed one across the table to Titus and lifted his glass to his lips.

Angelo held the heavy liqueur in his mouth for a full minute savoring the sweet licorice taste. After swallowing he smiled and said, "Your wife. I don't remember her name. She died leaving you with a little girl. A sad, sad thing. You still a cop?"

Titus' head moved slightly from side to side. "No," he said, deciding not to mention the sheriff badge he carried in his jacket pocket. He briefly explained Ann Marie's accident and her injuries, feeling a heaviness in his chest and his voice tighten as he explained that the incident was no accident. That she had been intentionally run off the road. That he suspected someone but could find no motive. That, when he could prove it he would deal with the man personally before turning him over to the authorities. And, that he suspected it had something to do with him and an unsolved murder that had happened last fall when he was still the town marshal.

"The murdered man was Carmine Valentino, Angelo. Tell me about Carmine Valentino."

The old man's eyes pinched closed, the creases across his forehead deepened. "Valentino?" he repeated. "You know, I don't remember so good anymore."

Of Mourning Doves and Heroes

Titus waited then said, "Dallas says you remember every puta, every thug in the city. You remember better than him. Better than anybody."

Angelo's face smoothed, his eyes twinkled. "Yeah," he said. "There was a family named Valentino over on Twenty-Eighth. The old man worked in the coal yard. His old lady was a shrew, a real nag. They had a couple a boys."

Titus leaned forward, folded his arms across the table. "Three?"

"Yeah. Yeah, three maybe. Forget the oldest one. Was crippled in Korea. Never came home to stay. In some kind of sanitarium I think. Carmine was the young tough, though. Made his bones early."

"Who was he connected with in the mob?"

Angelo's eyes settled on Titus, his mouth twitched. "This has only to do with my daughter, *pisan*," Titus assured him. "Nothing else."

Titus felt Angelo judging him. After a long moment he continued. "Carmine Valentino was a *capo* for the Paretti brothers when they were expanding their heroin and numbers business from the docks back in the early fifties."

Titus whistled softly. He remembered Vincent Paretti well. In retirement for at least the past ten years in Phoenix, the scar faced, hard jawed boss of bosses had still been considered an elder in the syndicate until his death a year ago. Could Vincent

Paretti have protected Valentino all those years? And if so, why?

"And it was in this capacity Valentino was hurt. In the line of duty, so to speak."

Angelo chuckled. "Yeah. He took a bullet meant for Paul Paretti in front of the Rivers Edge Lounge. Was the place still there when you were a cop?"

Titus shook his head. Urban renewal had set in. "Who was the shooter?"

Angelo waved both hands into the air. "There was a war on."

Titus sipped at his drink. "That was in fifty-seven, right?"

"Yeah, April. Until then each neighborhood had it's own hot shot that thought he run things. April and May and half of June of that year were real bad along the riverfront but especially in the flats area. Every two, three days a body'd turn up. Got so bad Giancana came out from Chicago to support the Parettis and stop the shooting. "Momo" had too much muscle to buck. The ones that didn't throw down left town."

Titus turned the glass in his hand, watching the heavy clear liquor coat the sides. If the intended victim was Paul Paretti, and Valentino was shot by mistake why would brother Vincent take care of Valentino for all these years? Unless--- "Could the shooter have been working for Vincent when Valentino got in the way?"

A cord in Angelo's neck tensed briefly, a tick pulsed rapidly at the corner of his mouth. The hand of reprisal from the *capa de tutti capo,* reached out to touch the white-haired old man even from the grave. "No," he said, bluntly. "That's not the way it was."

Titus let it drop. "What happened to Valentino, after?"

Angelo lowered his head. For a moment Titus wasn't sure Angelo was going to go on.

Finally Angelo spoke. "Someplace out of state to some kind of hospital, I think." He drained his glass. His tongue slipped out to touch his lips. The tension passed from his face, and he slipped back into remembering. "Never seen him after. Kind of too bad about him though, being hurt the way he was for a man the likes of Paul Paretti. The guy was a real bad number. In the spring of fifty-eight the Feds caught him on tape cutting up a hooker in a motel room. The DA wrote assault charges and the cops picked him up. A week later he disappeared from his cell in the city jail."

A smile tugged at Angelo's lips. "He was found in Toledo, neck tied."

Titus could guess what had happened. "So, brother Vincent had him killed before he could talk to the Feds."

Angelo didn't answer, instead he wobbled to his feet, used the cane to get to the cupboard then wobbled back with an ashtray and a black, twisted cigar. Titus' nose wrinkled involuntarily in anticipation; he hadn't smelled one of those in years. Soon a blackish cloud rose from around Angelo's head and radiated outward until it filled the kitchenette with the harsh acrid smell of burning rags.

"Ever hear the name Anthony De Gossi?"

"De Gossi," Angelo repeated. He set the smoking stogie in the ashtray and poured another finger full from the bottle. "No. Can't say I have. He the one hurt your daughter?"

Titus waved off a refresher. "His son. So far I can't prove it."

"S'pose to be from 'round here?"

"I don't know. Can't seem to find out. Even Dallas can't find anything." He leaned back in his chair running his finger under his collar. The room was getting warmer and the fumes from the cigar were finding a button in the pit of his stomach. He wished he'd grabbed a bite before looking up Angelo.

The old Don held the glass to his lips, savoring the heavy aroma and sweet taste. "Nope," he said. The glass chattered on the tabletop as he set it down. "Afraid you've stumped me. The son connected to the murder?"

Titus' chair scooted as he turned away from the table. "I can't find a connection. Its just Anthony Senior seems to have more pull than I gave him credit for, is all."

Titus pushed himself to his feet, went to Flori, took his hand. The bony fingers felt delicate and cool to the touch. "Thanks for the memories, *pisan*."

Angelo tilted his head up, his eyes twinkling. "Nah," he replied, flipping his hand. "I don't remember so good anymore."

Titus' lips curled into a twisted play-along smile. He looked down at the fragile body struggling to get to his feet, and reached his hand out, it was brushed away. "Maybe you should write a book before it's all gone," Titus said, with emphasis.

Angelo, leaning against the table, hiked his drooping trousers too high then fumbled for his cane and steadied himself before he looked up at Titus. He gave a quick tight laugh. "You want I should die before my time?"

"You are probably right," Titus answered, then pointed to the bottle of anisette. "Enjoy it in friendship. *Ameca*."

Angelo acknowledged Titus' praise with a flip of the hand and led the way to the door. In the doorway Angelo tapped Titus lightly on the arm with his cane. Titus turned. "This De Gossi," Angelo said. "He from the East Coast?"

Titus shrugged.

"You tell Dallas he should come around, I can still beat him at Pinochle."

*   *   *

Titus paused under the awning and zipped his jacket, running by what he had learned. It was not just that Carmine Valentino had past underworld connections but that he had been in the upper echelon of the local mob and evidently trusted by his hood cronies. Which brought up other possibilities: was he still involved? Was it a mob hit?   And Anthony De Gossi: was there a connection somewhere? What about an East Coast connection? Was Angelo trying to tell me something?

Titus jammed his hands in his jacket pockets and looked up. The sky was a stone gray; a fresh rain-slick glistened on the street. He picked out a dozen snowflakes riding the cold wind, turned up his collar, then headed for his car. If the roads were slick it would be well after dark before he got home.

-13-

T he light was still shining in Ann Marie's room when Titus slipped his key in the front door. Inside the living room, he fell into the chair and pulled his boots off, then checked the clock; eleven-fifteen. The usual two-hour drive had taken five hours over roads that had become sleet covered outside Jefferson City. He sat in the quiet, his head in his hands letting the burning in his eyes ease, listening to the wind whip the frozen drops against the window. A bolt of pain flashed down the back of his neck cutting across his shoulders. He straightened, rubbing the stiff muscles at the back of his neck. Between gusts of wind he heard voices coming from Ann Marie's room. Male voices. As always, the late night talk shows.

Titus got up from his chair finally and hung his jacket in the closet. After turning the heat up, he took something for the pain behind his eyes, then gently pushed her door open. His daughter, her eyes closed, was propped up on pillows. In the light from the hall the apparatus around her bed looked more like a cage.

He stooped, picked a book off the floor where it had landed after a bounce off the wall and set it on her nightstand then hit the switch on the radio. When the noise quit her eyes opened.

"What did you find out?"

The light from the hall revealed a tangled nest of dark hair framing her pale, puffy face.

"Not much. We'll go over it in the morning. I've got the makings of a horrendous headache."

"Okay," she sighed.

Her depression had lifted after she had come home from the hospital, now after a week it was coming back. He pulled the wheelchair aside and stepped close, touched her arm, then laid his hand on her forehead. He knew what a touch could do; pass love, strength, and understanding from him to her and back. Strengthening both. He knew because it always had. Since she was an infant. And he'd often wondered if he'd gained more than his precious daughter. Now he wished for it more so. "JoAnna called," Ann Marie said, the depression in her voice, evident.

"Thanks. I'll call her tomorrow."

"No you won't." Her voice had a hard, sharp edge. "She says she hasn't seen you in two weeks and hasn't talked to you in days. What's wrong? I thought the two of you were an item?"

"I haven't had time."

Ann Marie's bare foot slipped from the covers as she pushed herself upright. The bedspread fell to her lap, she leaned back on her hands and looked at him with a curious frown that gradually hardened. "That's a damn lie."

Titus ignored her comment. She wouldn't understand. How could she, he didn't understand, himself. "Did the Recovery Center call with next month's rehab schedule?"

Her face flushed and her nostrils flared but he knew she wouldn't press him. The silence stretched between them.

Finally she sighed, leaned back on her arms and answered, "Wednesday afternoon. After the new brace goes on."

"Fine. I should have the afternoon free. Afterward we'll stop for Chinese."

He watched his daughter's features relax, saw her chest heave beneath her nightgown. "Yeah," she replied wearily, and fell back on the pillow.

Titus thought of telling her about his visit with Flori but he was too tired. He'd tell her in the morning. "Goodnight, sunshine," he said, shutting off the light.

He heard her say, "Goodnight... Dad?" She stopped him in the doorway. "JoAnna is good for you. Think it over."

Titus pulled the door closed without answering.

*   *   *

A terrible wherring pain in her head stirred Ann Marie. She put her palms to her temples and squeezed, then opened her eyes. The room was pitch black yet that slight movement sent stabs of pain tearing through her head. She pressed her eyes tight and swallowed hard, her face twisted in agony. She sucked a breath, turned to the clock on the nightstand and slowly opened one, then the other. They wouldn't focus. She closed and opened them again. Alarm slackened her face as a heat flash crawled through her chest to her throat. I'm really sick, she thought.

Ignoring the sickening throb in the pit of her stomach, she sat up and again tried to bring the red digits of the clock into focus. The numbers remained a blurred red strip. She pressed her fingers to her eyes easing the savage pounding only slightly. I've never had a headache like this.

Her head slumped when she pulled her hands from her face. Something's wrong!

Of Mourning Doves and Heroes

She drew a deep breath flinching at the deep stabbing pain that cut through her lungs. Why does my chest hurt?

She sat still for a moment hoping the fuzzy feeling behind her eyes would go away then gave her head a quick shake sending a lightening bolt through the top of her head bringing out a weak cry. Burying her face in her hands she let a minute pass while the pain faded. This time she lifted her head slowly. A shiver began at the base of her spine and grew as it crept up and across her shoulders. God! I have to get to dad!

She threw the covers off, her hands found the bar over her head and she tried to turn. She couldn't move, her strength was gone. She weaved her fingers together and tried again. Her attention went to the brown pill bottles on the night table. A reaction from the pain medication!? She clamped her teeth and wrenched around. Her legs slipped from the bed, the brace on her left leg striking the wheelchair and skidding it away. She rested, fighting for air with the muscles of her stomach painfully tight. Beads of sweat broke under her ratted bangs. Her hand went to her mouth and a tremor shook her as a rush of heat swept up her neck. She swallowed hard then doubled over, retching through her fingers, over her legs to the floor.

She choked, lifted her head and wiped her face with the back of her hand. Her head was whirling. Her breaths were coming in quick fitful gulps. She forced her mind back. Before bed she had taken two tablets of the pain medication and the antibiotic. Fear tightened her throat. Had she taken more? Why couldn't she remember?

Unsteadily she reached for the bedpost, then the lamp switch. She looked down at herself. Her nightgown was bunched at her waist and disgusting. She pulled the wheelchair tight to the bed and reached for the overhead bar. I have to get to Dad, she thought.

She pulled herself up and with help of the nightstand she stood, steadying herself a moment. It came again, her body racked and another hot bolt rose through her throat, spilling down her front. The lamp became a blur, her head whirled and she fell back to the bed. When Ann Marie opened her eyes again the pounding in her head was worse. She tried to swallow, her tongue felt too thick, her breaths were coming in fitful gulps. She lay still for a moment listening. The lamp was moving, floating toward the ceiling, then she was gliding with it, slipping up, sinking. I have to get to that damn wheelchair and get out of here!

Slowly she pushed herself up, rolled and sat on the edge of the bed hanging on the overhead bar, her eyes pinched, her jaws clenched tight to keep the spinning from starting again. When her eyes opened they were stuck on the metal frame strapped around her left leg. A choking sob escaped, tears streamed down her face. "I want my legs back, goddamn it!"

She let out a sob, then another, then wiped her face on the sleeve of her nightgown and clutched the base of her throat. Get to Dad. If it's the medication, I need to get to the hospital.

"Dad! Dad!" She listened for a sound, a return call, hearing only the thumping in her ears. Her hand tightened on her throat, each wheezing breath seemed to add weight to her chest. "Dad!" she called again. Her mouth wouldn't work. She couldn't form the word. Got to get down the hall to Dad before I pass out.

She forced in a deep breath, tightened her grip on the side bar and stood putting her weight on the ungiving brace on the left leg. She fought to stand still, inhaling deeply, ignoring the pain, feeling the knot around her chest tighten with each breath. One turn and she would be in her wheelchair. She turned slowly, held in a breath and slumped back into the wheelchair. Now get out!

Her hands found the wheels, she pushed. In the hall Ann Marie's head cleared slightly, then she was at Titus' door. Sucking in a deep breath she pushed the door open and jammed the chair through. "Dad!"

She found the lights. Titus was curled up with two pillows. "Dad, something's wrong. I'm sick. Get up!"

She crashed into the table sending the lamp smashing to the floor. "Dad! Dad! Wake up, something's wrong!"

She pulled at his arm. "Oh my God, Dad! Wake up! We have to get out."

Titus didn't move. Fear struck deep into her breast. He couldn't be dead. She bent close and shouted his name into his ear, the effort drove a sharp pain deep into her lungs that nearly took off the top of her head.

She reached for the phone on the nightstand. Jabbing her finger at the tiny blur where the numbers would be. A clear female voice answered.

"Thisish Ann Marie Closson," she slurred. It was coming back. "Thwee need help."

"Can you give me your name again?"

"Ann Marie Closson!

"Ma'am, I am sorry, I can't understand you. Is there a problem at your home?

"Yes! Yes! Damn it!"

"Can you speak slower and clearer ma'am? What is the trouble? Is there someone else there with you?"

"Yes! My father!"

"Are you alone?"

Of Mourning Doves and Heroes

Ann Marie's hand was shaking. "No! I need a doctor!"

"Ma'am, don't put the phone down. Someone will be there shortly. Can you hear me ma'am? Stay on the phone. Can you hear me?"

She had to get him up. She set the wheelchair brakes. Gasping, she worked her hands under his head and tried to turn him but the strength was gone from her arms. She worked her way to the edge of the seat and leaned in. Then slipped her arms around Titus' neck and collapsed onto the bed.

"Ann Marie what's--"

She could feel a cool draft, then the sound of someone calling her name. A hand on her shoulder roused her. Slowly the blurred face of the person bending over her came into focus. "It's Titus, Tony!"

Marshal Tony De Gossi's gaze drifted down her wet, soiled nightgown. "Please, Tony," she pleaded.

As the sound of approaching sirens turned her head toward the window, Marshal De Gossi lifted her back into the wheelchair and pushed her toward the front door.

She sat in the open doorway shivering, letting the night chill clear her head, watching the rescue truck turn onto Panhandle Lane, swing into the drive and stop behind the Marshal's car. Two firemen scrambled out. She recognized one as Pete Jensen and shouted. "It's Titus, Pete. Please hurry!"

She turned back and pointed. "Down the hall."

The two firemen hurried in carrying large trunk-like black cases. In the distance she could hear approaching sirens. Leaving the door open she followed the two firemen through the house.

When Cliff Hensley came through the bedroom door, Titus was sitting up with his hands gripping the edge of the bed. A sheet covered his bare legs and a bedspread was draped over his shoulders fending off the cold blast coming from the two open windows. His head bobbed and weaved. He was mumbling behind the oxygen mask strapped to his face. Ann Marie, wrapped in a fireman's yellow coat, sat trance-like holding a mask, trying to keep the coat pulled closed while Pete Jenson checked her pulse.

"Ann Marie!" Cliff said. His eyes went from the her to Titus and back. "What happened?"

Slowly her head tilted back. He saw her ashen face. There was a blue shadow around her eyes, and her nightgown, protruding from the bottom of the heavy coat was wet with vomit.

She curled her left foot back and under her right ankle searching for a bit of warmth. "Sick, Cliff," she replied, her voice weak and resigned. She lifted her hand deliberately to her forehead and the front of the coat fell open. "Really sick."

Of Mourning Doves and Heroes

There was alarm in Cliff's voice. "Food poisoning?"

The fireman released her wrist and turned to the deputy, "I ain't sure, Cliff, but I could swear this looks like carbon-monoxide poisoning. We have to get them outside. I called for transport to Bergess General." He loosened the pressure cuff from Ann Marie's arm, folded the bulb into it and tucked it in the open case on the floor. "They'll need blood/gas work done to be sure but 'fore they return, the gas company'd best check out the heating unit in this house."

Tony De Gossi came into the room followed by the other fireman. He glanced around, spotted Titus, and spoke to the Deputy. "We checked around inside and out, couldn't see anything. No gas smells or anything. Probably a bug that's going around."

Pete Jensen shut the case, snapped the latches and with a grunt got to his feet. "Ambulance should be here in a bit." Lifting Ann Marie's hand he pressed her mask to her face. "Keep this on 'til they git here, young lady." He turned to the other fireman standing in the doorway. "Make sure the furnace's off, Jake." Then to the others, "If 'twas the heater, they both could 'ah died."

Cliff pulled the coat closed around Ann Marie, twisted a loop around a button, and touched her cheek. It felt cool. "I'll get it checked out," he said.

*   *   *

It was ten minutes past noon when Cliff Hensley saw the elevator doors open, got to his feet and stepped around the table of magazines. Ann Marie came out first in her wheelchair pushed by an orderly. Titus followed.

The Deputy caught Titus' hand. "Transportation on the county today, Ty."

"I talked to Sheriff Watkins earlier. Thanks."

Cliff turned to Ann Marie. Titus saw her frown smooth and a smile pull at the corners of her mouth. She set the brake and turned to the orderly. "This will be fine, thank you."

Cliff stepped forward. "I'll take it from here."

The orderly moved aside. Ann Marie shot the deputy a sharp glance then looked up at her father. "Come on. Let's get out of here." She clicked the brake lever off and gave the wheel a shove toward the door. While Titus stood watching, Cliff helped Ann Marie into the front seat of the cruiser. Then Titus settled into the back seat. When the door shut the deputy twisted around and poked a slip of paper through the metal screen to Titus, "Here is the plate check the sheriff ran."

Titus unfolded the paper. It contained the three plate numbers from last night and three names.

Of Mourning Doves and Heroes

Only one that he recognized--Leonard Barnes. He tucked it into his shirt pocket.

The deputy looked at Ann Marie. "Did you see or hear anything around the house last night?"

"She shook her head. "No. Nothing. Why?"

"There was nothing wrong with the furnace. The sheriff had a service check it out. I was there a while ago looking around. The heater vent pipe looked as though it had been plugged with something."

Titus sat up straight. "With what?"

The deputy's hand turned up, his head moved back and forth. "I don't know. I found your ladder and went up on the roof. The end of the pipe had been disturbed, scuffed up. You know what I mean? Like something had been stuffed inside then removed. No sign of what it was, though. I checked all around the yard."

Despite the sun beaming through the windshield Titus felt his face go cold. At the same time he heard Ann Marie's gasp. "Someone tried to kill us."

The deputy turned the ignition. A minute later he merged the cruiser into the light afternoon traffic on # I- 14.

Ross Tarry

-14-

JoAnna's fingers bit into Titus's forearm as the small commuter touched down with a squeaking, teetering dance, then settled onto the runway of the Southport Regional Airport. Within thirty minutes they had retrieved their two bags, rented a Ford and were driving along the low coastal plain of North Carolina.

After thirty years as the top crime reporter on the Boston Globe, there was nothing Nicholas Biscotti didn't know about the old East Coast mob., Dallas had explained. Being retired may have pulled him out of the current information loop but if anyone would know about the name De Gossi and a tie to the mob it would be Nicholas.

A picture book of the eastern seashore lay open on JoAnna's lap. "Oh! Pelicans, Ty. Look at them all."

The sun-bleached timber breakwater protecting an extravagant, walled-in brick house from the sea was covered with the large gray birds.

Asking JoAnna to accompany him on this trip to North Carolina to interview Nicholas Biscotti had not been an afterthought. His hope was to find just the right time, just the right surroundings to talk about the direction of their relationship. That he loved her was without doubt. He had been smiling inside since their trip to Jefferson City and their first night together. However, the part of him that had grown used to fulfilling his own wants at his discretion had become jealous at the intrusion of someone so soft and so able to steal his heart. If she was to remain a part of his life some guidelines needed to be set. A flutter tickled his throat. Opening up about these kind of feelings was something he wasn't sure he could do.

It had been a long four hour flight into Wilmington during which their conversation had been restrained. He presumed by the proximity of the other passengers. Then a crowded cabin in the small shuttle. Now they were alone. On the left, beyond an immense salt marsh studded with slate-gray pools of still water and clumps of stunted trees, the Atlantic rolled in cold and forbidding. Overhead the afternoon sun was a light spot in the high overcast.

Of Mourning Doves and Heroes

"We'll stop at the first decent motel we see," Titus said as they were driving over a hill. "And maybe something to eat. That flight food tasted like paste."

JoAnna smiled at him. "Sounds fine. Two rooms or one?"

Titus felt his ears redden, a sheepish grin pulled at his mouth. "I was hoping just one," he replied, glancing at her from the corner of his eye.

She was dressed in a classy pastel shift, showing smooth, tanned shoulders and a lot of brown, fit leg. Her teeth showed white through a bright smile. "I'm just teasing, Ty." She squeezed his arm, playfully. After a pause she said, "We need to be together. Not only for that---" her words hung in the air just long enough for a slight flush to color his ears. He turned his eyes from the road. She was looking down; her bottom lip was curled between her teeth, her face somber. She traced a circle on the seat between them. "We need to discuss you and me," she said.

The blush turned to a prickle of cold that slid across his shoulders. He swallowed hard and nodded. He had the feeling he was about to get dumped.

They found a strip motel, a row of ten wind-blasted units along the edge of a limestone covered parking area. Leaving their baggage on the bed in number twenty-seven they drove back up the road to Josie's for two bowls of chowder.

After he paid the check, Titus stopped at the phone and dialed his home number. He let it ring until Ann Marie answered. "Yes?"

"Hello, Sunshine."

Her voice brightened, "Hi, Dad."

Beside him JoAnna waited casually.

"Everything okay?"

"Yes. Cliff just stopped by. He's going to drive me in for my PT in the morning, then he says he'll stay until the on duty deputy arrives in the area." Her voice took on an irked tone. "At least the cops aren't sitting in the kitchen with me."

"We went all through this, Ann Marie. If Tony thinks he's being backed into a corner he will try again. Whether you like it or not, Ray Watkins is going to keep a deputy close by. Anything on that Monti Hammer?"

"Got his address. I'm trying to talk Cliff into taking me to Jefferson City to look him up."

Titus frowned. "Wait 'til I get back."

"If I can talk Cliff into it I'm going, Dad. Beats being pent-up in this house."

Titus shook his head. He had no business leaving her alone. Only at Dallas' urging had he decided to fly all the way to North Carolina to talk to Nicholas Biscoti.

He felt JoAnna's hand on his arm. "Anything else?"

"Something very interesting. My friend in the Clerk of Records office called. Carmine Valentino owned twenty percent of the Sun Dancer. After his death his share of the property went back to the group who owned the balance, Riverfront Land Management Inc. Guess who controls Riverfront Land Management?"

Titus cringed. "Vincent Paretti's old organization."

"Yes. If Carmine Valentino refused to agree to a sale, Tony De Gossi couldn't go through with his purchase."

"Sounds like we've got our motive." A sudden chill settled over Titus. "Sunshine, don't go anywhere alone and do what Cliff says."

Titus held the phone away from his ear for long seconds before placing the receiver back on the hook after Ann Marie clicked off. "Shouldn't have left her alone," he said with such dreadful heaviness it brought JoAnna's hand slipping around his waist. He looked at her. "Valentino had twenty percent interest in the Sun Dancer that reverted to the majority owners upon his death. My guess would be it was the old man's only income and when he refused to sell Tony De Gossi killed him."

"I don't know Tony De Gossi at all, Ty. But what you have told me about him, I would wonder if he would have enough pluck to kill someone. He sees himself as a big shot, but he's too loud. Too impulsive. Not very secure at all."

Titus cupped JoAnna's bare shoulder in his palm, slid his hand down the back of her arm. "Ann Marie was run off the road. The furnace vent was tampered with." He shook his head. The only one with a motive is Tony. No. Tony killed the old man. But I have nothing that places him there at the time of death. No witnesses. There has to be something." He turned to face the door. A young man in a loud shirt and shorts held the door for a pretty brunette carrying a sleeping infant.

As the young family passed, JoAnna grabbed Titus' hand. "Cliff is with Ann Marie. She will be fine. We've come a long way to talk to this man, Biscotti. We need to get going." She pulled on his arm. "There is something going on between Cliff and Ann Marie. He won't let anything happen to her."

Titus pulled his hand free and stopped. When JoAnna saw his face fall in astonishment the corners of her mouth turned up and she reached out and patted his cheek.

By four-thirty they had found the mailbox where he was told it would be, and the turnoff through the grass-tufted dunes. The two-story house at the end was the color of the sand dunes that surrounded and separated it from the sea; an architectural balance of concrete squares and sharp corners. Had the structure been large it would have spoke of opulence, instead it seemed a part of the seaside setting; itself an odd-shaped dune.

Nicholas Biscotti was a slight, fit man that looked to be in his mid-sixties. According to Dallas he was much older.

"Your name Closson?" the man called from the entryway.

Titus had circled around the front of the rental to JoAnna. "Titus Closson and this is JoAnna Stanford."

The sand was soft where the wind had piled a wide ridge across the boardwalk leading from the driveway to where the old man stood in the doorway. The air smelled of salt. From beyond the dunes Titus could hear the soft roll of the surf.

Nick Biscotti came to the rail, slipped the plaid porkpie hat from his head revealing a freckled dome with wisps of fine sandy hair, and reached out to JoAnna. "Pardon me ma'am, I missed your name." He patted his ear. "Age and the wind, you know."

Titus remembered Dallas' final warning as he helped with the luggage at the airport. He had grabbed Titus by the coat sleeve and nodded toward JoAnna. "Nickie Biscotti's charmed more women out of their drawers than any man I know of."

"JoAnna Stanford, Mr. Biscotti." Titus heard JoAnna's reply. He stamped his feet trying to knock the sticky sand from his shoes and maybe to tear Biscoti's stare from JoAnna. "Dallas sends his greetings," he added, kicking his shoes together.

Nicholas Biscotti's smiling face moved back and forth between them, lingering longer on JoAnna. "I was thrilled to hear from him. Kept in touch over the years, but it's been a while. Come in."

Nicholas' eyes settled on JoAnna while he stepped back holding the door. "This way," he said with a little bow, then reached a hand out for JoAnna's arm.

*   *   *

It was two hours later when Titus swung the rental back onto the narrow blacktop. The overcast sky was gone, the sun was a brilliant orb in the top corner of the windshield. He adjusted the sun visor and headed west to 917, one hand holding the wheel the other blocking the blinding rays sliding around the visor.

A dark pickup materialized out of the wavering heat rays at the crest of a hill. Titus squinted and gripped the wheel tighter. "What did you think of Mr. Biscotti?"

"Different. Not what I had expected at all," JoAnna replied, pulling a steno pad from her purse.

"Yeah. Not what I pictured either. Dallas said he knew the mobs better than any reporter in the country. But Biscotti blew Vincent Perretti off as an idiot. Either he doesn't know what he's talking about or he was just talking to put us off. We really didn't fly all the way out here for a history lesson on the Gambino family and the crooked politicians of the east coast."

JoAnna had paged through three pages of notes then stopped. "He did give us the name Angelo Degostini though."

"I caught that too." Titus shot an approving glance at her. "His face went kind of white when he saw you react. He knew you made a connection. What made you ask about mob connected accountants or attorneys?"

JoAnna pulled her shoulders back with the air of someone who had guessed at a long shot and been right. "Anthony De Gossi, if that is who he really is, was influential enough in the organization to be able to make a phone call and get his son out of a jam. Yet no one connected the name as a criminal. No police record has surfaced. I have been doing a lot of reading and finding some interesting things. These bigtime hoodlums were very adept at their version of public relations. Creating an aura of benevolence amid a whole class of people. Using ancestry, neighborhood, us against them, to build loyal support. And among these people were many professionals who worked entirely within the law for the various mob families."

Titus was smiling, his head moving up and down. Listening to her back there he had realized she had done her research. She had become a knowledgeable and cautious interrogator. She knew how to anticipate and phrase the right question to get a sometimes surprising answer. It had worked with the nurse, Caroline Bates and had worked again now. "Excellent deduction. But don't think in the past tense, that's the way it still is."

A motorcycle sat in the brown stubble of the shoulder at the base of a long sweeping curve that merged onto the main road. Titus slacked off the accelerator and moved to the left edge of the asphalt. Across the gravelly ditch its rider lay curled in the shade of a wide magnolia.

"You didn't like Mr. Biscotti very much, did you?"

He felt JoAnna's eyes pulling at him and he turned. The late afternoon sun highlighting her silver hair, softening the warm, fawn complexion of her cheeks and sent a burst of warmth through him that settled in his chest just above his heart.

"It showed?" he managed a murmur.

Of Mourning Doves and Heroes

"The man's a decent artist, especially his charcoals of the seashore."

Titus felt his muscles tighten the way they had when he was sitting across that low table from Nicholas Biscotti. "He thought you were pretty decent too, I guess."

"What do you mean?"

Titus flicked his eyes from the road to JoAnna and back. "The only time he took his eyes off your legs was when you got up to look at the paintings stacked along the wall. And then he couldn't take his eyes off your bottom."

Feeling JoAnna's stare he pulled his shoulders up and sniffed. He shouldn't have said that and her silence reinforced that conclusion.

He slowed for a two-block channel town of weathered single story buildings and a half dozen fishing boats tied along the quay. Ahead an ancient red dump truck turned onto the asphalt road chugging and spitting blue fumes that hugged the roadway. Titus settled in close behind, his mind on chiding himself for saying something so juvenile.

The truck slowed to a crawl then turned off into a dirt lot in front of a freshly painted blue building with a sign over the open door identifying it as the SQUAT and GOBBLE.

"Stop for dinner?" he asked.

JoAnna turned his way, her face scrunched in disgust. "I believe I will wait for Josie's, thank you."

Titus brought the rental Ford back up to speed. "Did we get anything else from Mr. Biscotti? Seems like mostly a wild goose chase to me."

"Nothing that I can come up with. Except, why would Anthony De Gossi change his name from Degostini?"

"If he did," Titus replied.

"You don't think he did?"

"All Biscotti said was there was a young attorney named Angelo Degostini who had worked for the Gambino's in Brooklyn."

"Do you think he gave us the name, intentionally?"

"No. He was rattling off names and it slipped out. He knew he'd made a mistake." Titus sighed. "I guess I expected more out of this trip. Something that would tie Anthony De Gossi in a different way to Valentino."

They were back in Holden Inlet now, and the traffic was getting heavier.

"Make up your mind!" There was the high tone of surprise in her voice. "Earlier you said Tony was the killer."

Titus' mouth twisted tight, it was a while before he answered. "He is, I'm sure of it. But, so far we have absolutely nothing except speculation. So far not a shred of physical evidence that would put Tony anywhere near the scene of the murder."

"And you are saying his father had something to do with it?"

"No. But lately I've had a feeling there is more to Anthony than anyone knows."

Titus put his signal on, slowed and turned east onto Town Mill Road. The only thing left of the sun was the wide gold-red band on the horizon. "All I've come up with so far is that both Valentino and Anthony De Gossi arrived in Lawrence about the same time. Which means nothing. I was hoping Nicholas Biscotti could add something."

*   *   *

Titus left enough on the table to cover the check plus a tip and followed JoAnna past the glass case of pastries into the entryway. He checked his watch, it was almost seven. Touching JoAnna's arm he said, "I'm going to call Dallas before it gets too late and give him the name Angelo Degostini. See if he can come up with anything."

She nodded in agreement. "I'll wait outside for you."

Titus dug a coin from his pocket and stopped to watch the glass door of the booth swing shut. She had been distracted through dinner, hardly responding to his attempts at conversation. He watched her standing in the circle of the street light looking up, her purse in her hand and her hands crossed in front of her. A grim sadness weighed heavy in his chest. What would it be like not to have her in his life? The truth was for the past two months she hadn't been out of his thoughts for more than a few moments at a time. Strange how he had forgotten, after all these years how fulfilling it was to love someone. What it did for the human spirit. He knew how Ann Marie's love touched him. In such a short time JoAnna had found a deeper, more vulnerable spot that had been left untouched since Sandra's death. He thought back to Tuesday afternoon at the accident scene and regretted his thoughts of wanting to be left alone, of feeling crowded. She had said, in the car, the two of them needed to talk yet insisted on one room. His love was growing stronger every day. What would he do if she wanted to keep the relationship light? He felt a lump swelling in his throat and his hand began to tremble.

He dropped the coin in the slot and punched in his card number. Leah recognized his voice and said Dallas had gotten a phone call and left shortly before eight. Titus gave her the name Biscotti had given them and the phone number at the motel. He inquired about their well being and hung up, deciding to wait to call Ann Marie before they left for the airport in the morning.

Of Mourning Doves and Heroes

The sounds and the ocean air came softly through the open window as the tires crunched to a stop in front of number twenty-seven. Titus switched off the engine. The smell of salt was heavy, the sky as dark and blank as a blackboard. Behind them the grumble and growl of the street traffic muffled the distant roll of the surf. A dozen rain drops, as big as quarters, pelted the windshield, then quit.

Titus hooked a finger around the door latch. He could feel JoAnna's eyes on him. Filled with misgivings, he was reluctant to look at her. Then did, bringing a smile to her face. "Not too late to get separate rooms, Jo."

"Not on your life!" She gave him a long steady look. "I have too much invested in tonight," she added in a much lower voice.

A small frown furrowed his forehead. She had obviously put much more thought into this trip and their relationship than he had. He swallowed with difficulty. Now he was sure he wasn't up to this night.

*   *   *

Titus steadied the two steaming plastic cups tightly in his fingers, slid the glass doors open with his elbow and stepped out onto the covered patio.

It was dimly lit in the static flicker of an electric imitation gas lamp hung from the right corner-pole.

JoAnna was seated on the oak and iron bench facing the ocean her arms and legs under a turquoise robe pulled to her neck. Her bare feet slipped from the fake driftwood log and the robe fell open to her lap as she turned to Titus and reached to take a cup from his hand. "Thank you." she said, her expression curious.

"Herb tea." There was a clue of smugness in his words. "Hope you like my choice."

The lamp flickered on her surprised face. "You? With herb tea?"

"I've found that motel coffee makers make better hot water than coffee."

The weak lamplight softened the sharp silver of her hair, darkening it and giving it a flaxen cast. It textured her cheek, the back of her hand and her leg that had slipped from the confines of the robe. Titus swallowed, wetting his throat. She had never looked so beautiful.

JoAnna lifted the cup, blew a delicate breath across the top and touched her lips to the rim. "Wonderful." She smiled and straightened, making room.

"Herb tea is one of those things I've tried over the last months since we've been seeing each other that I find I enjoy." Titus squeezed in beside her, aware of the light flowery scent of her perfume and the warmth of her body.

Her mood deepened as she looked away, holding the cup of tea in both hands as though fighting a cold wind. "What an interesting segue for what we need to discuss."

"Jo." He scraped the sand from his throat. "I thought we got on well together. If there is something I've done or said--"

"No. Nothing like that. And we do get along quite well."

He felt the pressure in his temples ease a notch, maybe this wasn't as serious as he thought. After all, she had made a point of wanting to spend the night together.

"I used to feel guilty, when Wagner was alive, about the feelings I had. Oh, Wagner was a good man. And I had my daughter and my home, but my life had this strange empty feeling. And I didn't know why or what to do about it. Then after Susan went off to school, that corner of me grew until I didn't know myself any more at all." Her words ran down to a pensive silence. After a moment she sipped her tea and continued. "I went on what I would describe as a quest. That's when I went back to school and got re-certified. I did volunteer work and took art classes. Wagner disapproved. He couldn't understand why I wasn't happy just being with him. Even after he died it took a while.

Several years, but I like the woman I found. I am a real individual, not a part of another person."

He heard the change in her voice. "Some of those negative feelings are coming back again," she said.

Titus' hand closed around her arm. "Jo, I haven't---"

"Please," she cut him off and pulled her arm free. "Let me continue."

"You are afraid of me," she said, after a pause. "I can feel it when we talk."

"Afraid?"

"Yes. Ty, I love you and you know that. And I know you love me, but I don't want to be married to you. Not now anyway."

Married! He felt his face redden, felt heat surge around his neck. They had never spoken of marriage though he'd certainly thought of it. Had she been expecting a proposal? Of course! That's the way it works. The woman gives her body, and expects marriage to follow. "Jo, maybe it is time to talk about it."

She turned her head away from him. "Ty. Will you pleeease listen?"

Titus' mouth fell open as she stood and moved across the patio and leaned against the cornerpost. Suddenly their separation of feet seemed like miles.

Of Mourning Doves and Heroes

"You are a gentle creature, Ty. We talk and talk and talk." Her voice was soft, barely above a whisper. "You seem totally open with me. But I sense you holding back. We need to be open with each other Ty. Listen to each other. I won't have it any other way."

Titus felt the anxiety slipping. His face relaxed into a half-smile. This was something that would pass, something he could deal with. Reassurance. It wasn't the serious break he had feared. The bench creaked as he rose and held open his arms.

The glint in her eyes exploded into flame. Her hands came up in a barrier. "Damn you! This is not trivial! It is the most important discussion we will ever have, because ---"

He stopped cold and watched her take a deep breath, watched the heat in her face quickly dissipate and the deep lines fanning out from the corners of her eyes, smooth. She slowly let her arms fall. She had obviously planned her words and wasn't going to let a flash of temper change the direction.

"I have my home, Ty. My work. You have a home and Ann Marie, for now at least. I am going to tell you what I want from you and what I can give. Then you will decide if you can be that person."

He watched her in amazement, listening intently because he knew if he didn't she would know instantly.

"I want a soul friend. Someone who will share my life with me. Someone who will listen and respond; talk openly and honestly. That I love you is without question. That I hold you as a dear and true friend is without question. But I must have that feeling from you. I don't get it. You stayed away for two weeks without saying why and never explained. I assume you needed time alone."

"That wasn't it." But he knew it was.

Her nostrils flared for an instant, her eyes tightened in a piqued look then went flat. "I know the feeling Ty. I would have understood."

She paused and he felt her searching his face. The reflection of the lamp made a fiery sparkle in the mysterious dark centers of her eyes that seemed to reach to an unimaginable depth. And in that depth, to his surprise Titus saw a twinge of fear. As he watched they welled and glazed. Then he realized this ultimatum she was giving him was a challenge to see her as she saw herself and her fear was the fear he wouldn't.

She turned away for a moment then turned back fully composed. Her gaze drifted up. "Secondly, I want a lover. To explore and to explore me."

The erotic tension that was always present between them, spiked. A thumping sensation

Of Mourning Doves and Heroes

started in his cheek and he fixed his gaze to the dark sea beyond. Was this a test to see if she was reaching him? He felt a quickening in his stomach.

Finally her gaze slipped off to the side. "Wagner wasn't much in that area. It took being widowed at fifty and alone to find that part of me. You have already proven yourself."

His lips set hard in a stiff awkward smile. The tightened muscles in his face stopping the twitch in his cheek. When she looked back she was smiling. She reached up and touched his face, her fingers lingering. "Sometimes I get wet just thinking about you and I didn't think that was supposed to happen to a woman my age."

Titus felt the familiar heat growing in his loins, his neck was getting warmer. Over her left shoulder he saw the black sea rolling in on white phosphorescent crests. The moon had poked through somewhere off to the right.

Titus lifted his arm to draw her to him. "Jo, We---."

She pushed him away. "Just let me finish. Because if we don't get this out their won't be a we. Between us there can be only trust with no doubts, love with no doubts and honesty about our feelings. Without this understanding between us there can't be anything. I have too much invested in myself."

Her words and voice came through clear. Strange how the word doubt hit such a strong cord. It had been the whisper he'd been hearing for weeks. Doubt that these feelings that had filled his heart were real and would last.

Suddenly all the doubt was gone. He put a finger to her chin and lifted. "I have too much of my heart invested in you to let you go, Jo. I may need some coaxing, but after witnessing your skill at getting people to open up, you should have no trouble with me."

Her mouth curled up showing a white toothed smile. He slipped his hand around her waist. "When you came back into my life you brought something too extraordinary to let pass."

She sighed and leaned against him, her hair brushing his face and her scent filling him. He folded his arms around her. And when she pressed back he felt the tightness go out of his body. He had made it over this hurdle and would make it over all the others.

She held on for long minutes, the heat of her breath on his neck fanning his desire to an obvious presence. Then she placed a kiss on his cheek and leaned back.

"Now let's celebrate this new openness," she said, stepping back. Her fingers slipped down his arms to his wrists. She lifted his hands, put them together and touched them to her lips. "After, we will talk more." The smile that slid across her face sent a faint shudder through Titus' bones. The real test was yet to come.

*   *   *

She came across the bed to him. Her skin held the scent of lilac and it made his heart pound. Her sex felt vibrant and hot. Her urgency drew away years as if drawing sands back into the top of the hourglass. When they finished they lay in each other's arms and laughed an easy, happy laugh.

The brilliance of the moon reflecting off the glass-covered print of a vase of flowers lit the far corner of the dark room. JoAnna had her head on Titus' shoulder and, he had his left arm around her. They talked of commitment and respect, of loyalty and faithfulness, of times past and the future. And no he wouldn't be driving her to hair appointments and no she wouldn't be washing his underwear. Gradually the pauses between the spoken thoughts and confessions grew longer until just as their breaths came in synch the phone jarred them back.

Reaching for the light with one hand JoAnna tucked the phone against his ear and curled around to the foot of the bed, her legs folded, listening.

"That's okay, Dallas. It's no problem."

Titus listened a moment then sat up and leaned back on his left arm. "Really. If it's the same man, we now know a lot more about our Mr. Anthony De Gossi than anyone ever imagined."

JoAnna crawled off the bed, picked up her robe from the chair and swept it around her bare shoulders.

Titus grabbed his watch from the lampstand and held it to the light. "It's after midnight, there. Wait until morning."

He swung his legs over the edge of the bed and dropped the watch back to the table. "Okay, but I'm sure Leah would be happier if you waited."

A grim frown came over his face, he nodded once. "Well, just be careful, *pisan*. This is the old-line mob were talking about not some young thugs."

Titus cradled the receiver and stared down at the weak circle of lamplight, reluctant to lift his hand from the phone. A tiny germ of warning inside his head was trying to make enough noise to get through. He was relieved when JoAnna spoke. "What was that about?"

He turned his head slowly up to meet her curious look. He was worried about Ann Marie. Now Dallas. And so overwhelmed with love for this woman standing before him. Everything felt so jumbled together. Too small of a basket for so many apples.

He pushed the phone back and sat with his elbows on his knees. "In the early fifties an Angelo

Of Mourning Doves and Heroes

Degostini worked for an investment brokerage firm. Swisher, something and something. His wife was somehow connected to the Bonanno family. The SEC uncovered some discrepancies in the books and this Angelo Degostini testified against the directors. They went to jail. The Bonanno's put new directors in and Angelo Degostini disappeared."

JoAnna sat on the edge of the bed, left foot on the floor, right foot pulled back against her bare leg. "With a new identity and a large amount of mob money, probably."

"Maybe enough to start a small town bank and live a nice respectable life."

"But what does that have to do with Carmine Valentino?"

"Nothing, but it explains how he could make a phone call and get his son out of a jam with the law."

"Do you think he could have something to do with the Sun Dancer?"

Titus shook his head. "It would surprise me if he did. Anthony is a bit snooty. He's a successful businessman and has the respect of the community. He likes playing the role. Drives a big foreign car. Lives in a modest but nice home."

He stopped for a thoughtful moment. "I've known the man for over twenty years. I couldn't imagine him being involved in anything that would color his reputation. He's even a bit of a philanthropist. No, he'd do what he could to keep his troubled son out of a jam, but there would be a limit."

JoAnna had come around to the other side of the bed, dropped her robe on a chair and slid under the sheet. "It's no crime to be a successful banker."

"No. And so far we have absolutely nothing to tie Tony to Valentino's place at the time of the murder. In fact we have nothing except a damn good motive."

"You said wait until morning. What was that about?"

Titus' shoulders rose as he inhaled, he trembled as it went out. "Dallas had a call from someone who said he knew something about Valentino. Someone who wanted to meet tonight."

He felt JoAnna's hand slide up his back. In a few hours they would be on a plane. He slipped in beside her, the warm softness of her legs against his rekindled the coals of earlier. Propped on one elbow he kissed her on the nose, then nuzzled his way down her neck. "Would you like to sleep?"

"We can sleep on the plane," she answered threading her fingers through his hair, her breath catching on the last word as the pull of his mouth at her breast wrung a moan from her throat.

-15-

Titus drove steadily, his hands square and taut on the wheel, detached from the occasional squawk of the police radio. He tore his thoughts from Ann Marie and glanced down at the folded morning edition of the Jefferson City Sentinel on the seat between them. He couldn't believe the bold type. "Retired Officer Found Slain."

A phone conversation with a Lieutenant Romeo from the pay phone at the airport hadn't disclosed any more than the newspaper had. Dallas Massley had been found shot to death behind Roxy's Bar on Eighty-Third Avenue. Two blocks from the Seventh Street pier.

JoAnna stared out the window. "Poor Leah."

"What am I going to say to her?" With the end of his words came a long silence. He recalled Dallas when they were partners working the flats, and Dallas telling him one night as they began their patrol, how he had gone back to their apartment for something and found Leah on her knees praying.

JoAnna's hand on his arm pulled him from his reverie. "I would come with you when you see her, if you would like."

Titus swung out and around a piece of slow moving farm machinery before he gave JoAnna a nod. "If he had only mentioned the person's name he was meeting."

At Diamond Crossing he slowed and turned left on County Road Sixty-One. Twenty-five more miles. He would call Ann Marie from JoAnna's.

"Jo. Let's start from the top. Carmine Valentino drowns in a water filled ditch in a half-assed attempt to make it look like an accident. This man Valentino owns a share of a nightclub with a rough reputation that Tony De Gossi wants to buy. Next, Ann Marie is forced off the road. She had been looking into Tony's trouble at the State Patrol Academy. The only thing she can remember about the vehicle is a bright flash. Like a camera flash."

"I didn't hear about a flash?"

"That was the last thing she saw before she hit the bridge. Then Ann Marie and I are both nearly killed in our sleep by carbon monoxide after you and I interviewed Carol Bates. Now Dallas is murdered. He also checked Tony's record at the

Academy and uncovered this thing about an Angelo Degostini. One or the other got him killed."

"If Tony is the murderer like you think, we can't prove it unless we can place him at Carmine's."

"You are still not sure he killed Valentino are you, Jo?"

"Remember, Dallas said the director of the Patrol Academy told him Tony's psychological profile did not conform to the patrol's requirements."

"Sure," Titus replied. "He said Tony was a hotheaded screwball. How does that fit in?"

"Carmine's murder was cold and calculating."

"So he had help. Jamie Bender maybe."

"Maybe. But for the life of me I can't come up with a plausible theory on how everything is connected. Now your friend Dallas is killed."

Titus slowed at the bridge approach. Rust colored leaves clung defiantly to the scrub oak Ann Marie's car had plowed into. The yellow scars had paled and dried. The ruts in the earth had long since washed out. "I'd feel a lot better if Ann Marie had answered the phone."

JoAnna had kicked her left shoe off and turned to face him, her arm across the back of the seat. He felt a small measure of the distress at not being able to reach Ann Marie this morning, lift as JoAnna's fingers traced tender patterns over his shoulder and the back of his neck. "Ty," she asked after a moment. "Do you remember seeing that janitor at the airport?"

Until he let his breath out he hadn't realized he'd been holding it in. "I don't remember a janitor."

"After we dropped the rental off we crossed the street to the terminal."

Titus was shaking his head.

"There was a man by the taxi stand emptying a waste container. It was square. One of those yellowish ones that look like they are made of tiny yellow pebbles. The cover usually lifts off and the trash bag goes inside."

"I know the kind."

"Well this one had a conical shaped cover with an oval hole in each side. Like a Japanese lantern top."

Titus was staring at JoAnna.

"The top swung to the side to get the plastic bag out."

His mind had spun to the Japanese lantern sitting in the rubble of Valentino's house when his pager went off, flashing his home phone number.

JoAnna picked the car-phone from the hook, her finger poised over the number pad. "What do I do?"

"The pound sign twice, then the number."

Of Mourning Doves and Heroes

The speaker beeped the number back, then rang once. The answering voice brought a startled look to Titus' face.

"Titus. God, I'm glad I got to you." Cliff Hensley's voice was frantic. "You on the radio phone?"

Titus grabbed the phone from JoAnna's hand. "Yes! Where's Ann Marie! What's wrong?!"

"Stop someplace and call back." The phone went dead.

Titus felt the chill that had draped itself around his shoulders slide down his spine.

The sun, exceedingly brilliant in the crisp, cold blue November set the hillside stands of port-colored sumac to blaze. Titus crossed the centerline, straightening a curve in a squeal of tires. Beside him JoAnna's breath came in stops and starts.

"I'll call from here," he said jamming the brakes and skidding through the dirt parking lot in front of Judy's Towing.

With JoAnna trailing, Titus burst through the door. "I need to use your phone!" He spun the counter phone around and franticly punched the buttons.

"Cliff what is it?"

"Ann Marie isn't here."

Titus was suddenly stone cold. The muscles in his arms trembled. His breath wouldn't come and when it did, it came as a moan from that deep, secret place where his worst fears are kept.

"I came to take her to her PT."

"She could have gone with someone else," Titus said, hoping it was true.

"Not without her wheelchair."

Titus' heart stilled. The air in his lungs came out in an unconstrained groan and his left hand went to the counter to brace himself as the blood drained from his legs. He thought he was going to fall.

"Ty!" JoAnna's shout was filled with alarm.

The strength of her arm as it slipped around his waist somehow kept his legs from folding.

The phone fell away from his ear. His head turned to JoAnna, agony filling his face. "Tony's got Ann Marie," he said, weakly.

"How?"

Cliff's clipped voice was coming from the phone. Titus straightened, the terror stampeding inside, controlled under taut muscle. He jerked the phone back to his ear. "Tony is crazier than we thought, Cliff. I'll meet you at the Sun Dancer. I'm five minutes away."

Titus had the door open before the car had come to a complete stop beside a black Cadillac. "That's Jamie Bender's car. You stay here."

"Not on your life!"

He had one foot on the ground, his hand on the top edge of the door. He looked back at her.

Bender and Hank were inside. They would know where Tony was, and he wasn't going to waste any time with either of them. "Stay in the car, JoAnna."

She lunged across the car for his arm. "Ty, wait for Cliff."

He pulled loose from her grasp. "Tell Cliff I'm inside."

Defiantly she reached for his hand. "You are not going in there without me!" Her eyes challenged him.

"JoAnna, I'm a cop. You're staying here!"

A brilliant circle of light danced over the side of her face striking her eyes. She lifted her hand to shield the beam and pulled back. "Ty. In that car. The light!"

Titus ducked down to follow her finger pointed through the windshield. A glass medallion hung from the mirror of the Cadillac, reflecting a blaze of sunlight through the side window.

His look moved quickly between JoAnna and the car.

"The reflection of her headlights before she hit the bridge. It had to be Bender's car," she whispered.

Titus felt his anger flair to a rolling boil. "He's in there. I'm going after that bastard."

Titus took the steps two at a time, hesitated for an instant to loosen the gun in his holster then slammed through the door. He let his eyes sweep the room. It was empty except for Hank bent over behind a bar lined with dirty glasses. Hank lifted his head enough to catch Titus' eye then shrank back when Titus took the dozen steps to the corner of the bar. "Where is Jamie Bender and Tony, Hank?"

Hank shook his head, his bald pate glistening in the sunlight streaming through the front windows, then jumped when Titus brought his fist down hard enough to make the glasses clink together.

"Tony's a mad man, Hank. And he's got Ann Marie. Now tell me where he and that Bender are!"

Hank took a step back. His hands were shaking and his eyes flickering frantically around the room. The beads of sweat forming on the mass of forehead broke, running in streams down the round red face.

His lips trembled. "Mmmarshal, I don't---." The click of a latch and the creak of a wooden board drained the blood from Hank's face. Titus stared at the green door in the corner. The cellar! There is an outside entrance in the back! Titus bolted for the front door, reaching for his gun. He took the steps in three strides and swung around the bottom rail post as JoAnna came running from behind the car door.

"Stay back!" he shouted. Running, he half turned, "When Cliff gets here tell him to cover the cellar door from up there!"

Of Mourning Doves and Heroes

With his heart thudding in his ears, Titus gripped his gun in both fists, raised his arms and kicked out, catching the door with the flat of his boot. The door splintered at the latch and slammed open, flooding the cement block cellar in daylight. Tony De Gossi whirled away from the stairway, leveling a gun, twisting the chair with a bound and squirming Ann Marie around in front of him.

"Closson! I'll kill her! I swear I'll kill her!"

Titus froze in the doorway in a slight crouch. Where was Jamie Bender? His finger tightened on the trigger. Ann Marie twisted furiously against the duct tape that held her wrists to the arms of a wooden chair. More of the silver tape crisscrossed her chest and a short piece covered her mouth.

The muscles around his stomach twisted and hardened trying to keep the fury inside. "Where's Bender, Tony?"

Crouched behind Ann Marie, the white forehead of Tony De Gossi glistened in the gray light that filled the small dank room.

Titus could feel his heart thumping in his throat. His eyes moved quickly over Ann Marie. Her eyes were wide and bright, her face twisted with fury as she fought against the bonds. Sit still! his mind whirled. For God sake, sit still!

"Ann Marie!!" His shout stopped her. He saw the frenzied fear in her eyes change to trust, then calculation. She was the daughter trusting her life to him. The flames of fear leapt hot in his belly.

He took a deep, measured breath praying his thoughts would clear. The trembling slowed. Adrenaline rushed through his brain and everything snapped into sharp focus. The smell of empty beer bottles, the beer cases stacked to the beams of the cobwebbed ceiling, the high window on the right wall and the wooden stairway to the upstairs. The tendons in his outstretched arms twitched. Tony wouldn't leave his shield of Ann Marie to move for the stairway and there was no other way out except straight through the door.

"Lay the gun on the table, Tony. Then step away from Ann Marie." Titus fought to keep his voice calm. Bender could be hiding anywhere.

De Gossi turned his gun to the back of Ann Marie's head and crouched lower. "Stay back!"

The muscles in Titus' hands hurt. His heart was banging. He was going to watch his daughter die. The trembling in his chest rose into his throat. "Where is Bender?"

Tony's eyes were ready to pop from his head. "The gutless prick run out!"

"Put the gun on the table, Tony."

De Gossi jabbed the gun against Ann Marie's ear starting a trickle of blood. "You two are not going to ruin this for me, Closson."

Of Mourning Doves and Heroes

Titus' trembling hands tightened around his gun. Just a fraction of a second. Just an instant. He looked into the taut twisted red face of Tony De Gossi. The bulging eyes were glistening, and mad. Killing was going to happen. Tony De Gossi. Him. But please, not Ann Marie.

"This place is going to make me rich. Hear me?"

Titus forced his breath even. Sweat ran out of an armpit and tickled its way down his ribs. "Your head is all messed up, Tony. It's over. Put the gun down." He forced the words out slow and clear. "You don't want to hurt Ann Marie."

Ann Marie lunged against the bonds and snorted through the tape, jarring the table beside her. Tony made an unintelligible bawling noise and twisted his hand in Ann Marie's hair, jerking her head back. "I'll kill her. I mean it! You're going to make me kill her!" The man's face was blood red, his lips were pulled back over his teeth. His eyes were flashing back and forth.

"Then you will have to kill me, too. And Ray Watkins knows I'm here. Knows you're here. You've already killed twice, Tony. That's enough."

Tony yelled, much louder than necessary. "I never killed anybody."

"Sure you did. You killed Carmine Valentino, Tony. Wouldn't he agree to sell the Sun Dancer?"

Tony eyes shifted frantically around the room. "I didn't kill that old man!"

"Yes you did. And you killed Dallas Massley to keep me from finding out about your connection with the Jefferson City mob. Dallas was a friend of mine, Tony." The gun was getting heavy in his hand. The tip began to shake.

Tony's face was near purple. The sweat beads streamed down his cheeks. "I didn't!"

Titus' mind spun. Keep him talking. He'll give you an opening. Just, please turn the gun away from her for an instant you punk. Just for an instant.

"They're going to strap you to a gurney and stick a needle in your arm, Tony. Don't kill again."

Titus bit down on his lips, the knots in his legs tightened painfully.

Tony's T-shirt was darkening with sweat. Suddenly his face opened in a wide, mad grin. "You know Closson, you make me laugh. You can't stop me. I'll kill your precious daughter if you try. So just back away and let us get by."

"You can't take her with you. You crippled her, remember?"

Ann Marie's eyes caught his. Titus tried to make his stare tell her to be still. He saw her eyes lock on the corner window behind him, then down to the floor. He saw her foot move. Her toe inching toward the table leg.

Of Mourning Doves and Heroes

"I warned her. She wouldn't quit her goddamn snooping around. I had to show her I meant business."

From the corner of his eye Titus saw movement at the window, then saw Ann Marie take a deep breath and lunge. The table slid. The window shattered. Tony's gun swung to the sound. Titus held his breath and squeezed the trigger.

The sharp blast sent Ann Marie's head down. Then came the whoosh of exhaled breath as Tony De Gossi dropped with a flat thunk on the hard floor, his back against the side of the stairway, a blue spot on the broad forehead above the right eye.

Titus, frozen in a crouch, was looking past Ann Marie to the man on the floor. The single flat gunshot had sounded like the smack of a gavel in the close cellar, recording itself in his conscience and it seemed to have surprised Tony De Gossi by the look on his face, or maybe it was the surprise that death had come so quick.

Titus was lowering his gun, wary that Bender was around somewhere, when JoAnna burst through the door. Dropping something at his feet she rushed to embrace Ann Marie. Bender had escaped up the stairs to the Sun Dancer.

The fingers that had gripped his throat began to ease. He allowed himself a breath and straightened.

The pounding in his chest gradually slowed, he holstered his gun and knelt beside Ann Marie.

"Thank God you're all right!" JoAnna was saying as she gently peeled the tape from Ann Marie's mouth and went to work on one wrist.

Tears of relief washed down Ann Marie's face. Titus tipped her chin up with his fingers and wiped them away with his other hand. "It's okay, Sunshine. It's okay."

She tried to speak but the words percolated in her throat as a convulsive sob gripped her.

"It's all over, Sunshine. It's all over, now."

Titus felt her trembling, ease.

"I dosed off on the sofa. I heard someone---." Again, a sob choked her words. She took another breath. "When I turned the latch he kicked the door open. Tony was crazy, Dad. You should have seen his face. Screaming about us ruining things for him. He had a towel in his hand. The next thing I remember I was here."

JoAnna pulled the last of the tape from Ann Marie's right hand. As Ann Marie reached for Titus her tears gushed again.

"It's okay, Sunshine," he consoled her. He brushed her disheveled black hair back and held her face against the soft part of his shoulder letting her tears soak his shirt. When her trembling slowed he pulled back and was holding her wet face in his hands when a sheriff's cruiser slid to a stop in the dirt.

"Ann Marie!" Cliff's cry was anguish choked. He bolted from the car and through the doorway, nearly toppling Titus in his rush to Ann Marie. "My God! You're okay!" He held her by the shoulders.

"Yes. Yes." She was nodding, teardrops dripping from her chin.

Titus pulled himself to his feet, feeling strangely wobbly. "Let's get her outside."

Cliff helped JoAnna pull the last of the tape from Ann Marie's legs then stood and bent over. Ann Marie's arms went around his neck. He picked her up from the chair and carried her through the door.

Titus looked back at Tony. Years ago, patrolling the Jefferson City flats, he had been regularly haunted by the prospect of killing. He hadn't faced that thought in years. Now, suddenly it had happened.

Outside, Cliff set Ann Marie onto the trunk of the cruiser. She clung to the deputy, a small bundle curled in his arms, her head buried against his chest. Suddenly in Titus' mind he pictured a dark haired girl, an overturned bike, a tearstained face. The fluttering in his stomach turned heavy. How close he had come to being left with only memories of his daughter. He felt JoAnna move close and take his hand. Her voice was soft as she said, "I don't know who is more blessed, Ty. You, Ann Marie or me."

His scan of the tiny dank room stopped at the body of Tony De Gossi crumpled against the stairway. "It makes you wonder what he was blessed with." He slipped an arm around JoAnna and started for the door. If there was remorse it would come later.

Stopping in the doorway he picked his baton from the floor. "I found it in the back seat," JoAnna said.

He looked from JoAnna to the nightstick in his hands and back.

"I came around the other side and was listening. He was mad and desperate. Any second and he would have killed you." JoAnna's bottom lip began to tremble, a look of anguish came over her face, then was gone. "I was afraid I was going to lose you. I didn't think. I just swung as hard as I could at that window."

Titus pulled her to him, felt her arms tighten around him and felt a shudder roll through her. After a moment he tipped her head back with his fingers and traced a tear back to the corner of her eye with his thumb. Her mouth was drawn in a tight line, the corners of her lips twitched. "I love you," he said softly. Her arms grew tighter around him and he felt she was drawing something from him. Then it was coming back strangely comforting. It dawned on him that she had said a silent prayer. "Thank you," he whispered.

Titus went to the Cruiser, radioed the dispatcher, giving a description of Bender's car and license tag number.

When he finished he tossed the transmitter on the seat. From where he was standing he could see into the cellar; the wooden chair, the body of Tony slumped against the stairway. He looked around to see Ann Marie and Cliff locked in an embrace. How was it that the lives of two people could turn out so differently? Both Tony and Ann Marie had lost their mothers at the age of seven and were raised by a single father. It hadn't been an easy role, being both mother and father. But it had its rewards. With no competition for affection and attention, each knew the other's devotion to be total. That unquestioned knowledge between the two of them had allowed space for trust to grow. A sacred faith that one would always be there for the other. He had felt it as a pleasant pain that touched him anew each day for nearly twenty years. And even when she was a child he had taken comfort in seeing this trust in him as a sparkle of warmth in her eyes.

What had life been like for Tony? He had known Anthony to be a caring, involved parent; on the school board, Celebration of Harvest Days coordinator, sponsor of the softball team. Titus' brow's lifted. "You're right, JoAnna. And that is all we have been seeing through this whole investigation, the surface. Looking for the motive. The motive is there all right. Hidden in a stone vault, the Japanese lantern. But the man who killed Valentino didn't have a motive. He had a debt to repay."

Cliff Hensley looked puzzled.

"Tony didn't kill Carmine Valentino or Dallas," Titus said. "He ran Ann Marie off the road to scare her. He got desperate and tampered with our furnace. But he wasn't capable of looking someone in the eyes and coldly killing them. But I know who did."

-16-

With the even crunch of leaves under his feet, Titus moved quickly through the park to the old relic of the tank. His eyes were locked on the red brick house across the street. He slipped his gun from beneath his coat and trotted across the leaf-scattered pavement and up the smooth gray steps and stopped. The door was ajar. Anthony De Gossi had nowhere to go.

Titus eased the door open and slipped in, keeping his back to the wall. "Anthony? It's Titus, Anthony."

A chair creaked off the foyer. "In here, Ty."

Titus moved lightly into the parlor. The afternoon sun breaking through the big oaks, poured dark, irregular splotches across the light carpet, over the elegant sofa, and up the wall.

The door to the office was open. Titus could see the leather chair and the window. "Anthony?"

"It's okay, Ty. Come on in."

Titus gripped the gun, angled it toward the floor and stepped into the doorway.

Anthony De Gossi was turned toward the window in the high-backed chair, slouched forward, his elbows on his knees. The beam of sunlight pouring through the windowpanes turned the fine, white hair into a silver mantle. As he swiveled around Titus could see the heavy folds of weak skin above the tight collar of his custom-made shirt. His eyes were dull, his face drawn.

"Tony is dead, Anthony," Titus said, focusing on the man's face. It was hard to imagine Anthony De Gossi giving up.

"I know. I heard." The chair creaked as Anthony turned and stood, his back to Titus.

"Let's just walk out to the car. By then Ray Watkins will be here. No commotion. No nothing."

When Anthony turned back, Titus' heart flipped. De Gossi had a gun in his hand.

"Don't!" Titus' gun came up as he shouted.

Anthony's hand stopped, the gun pointed out to the side.

"Don't do this, Anthony." He had just killed the son. Now the father was facing him. "Lay the gun on the desk. There's no need."

Anthony took a step toward the desk and teetered. He reached to the back of the chair to steady himself.

Of Mourning Doves and Heroes

"Just put it down, Anthony!"

Keeping the gun pointed to the far corner, Anthony sat on the edge of the desk, his shoulders sagging before he pulled himself up straight. "We both lost our young wives and raised our children alone, Ty. You know how it was."

"Put the gun down, Anthony."

"Ann Marie turned into a fine young woman. Tony was all right too. But there was something missing in him. Something to hold him together."

"You killed Valentino, Anthony. I know why and how." He felt De Gossi look at him for the first time. "When you went to discuss the funding for the alarm system he wanted to install, you switched the medication his nurse had laid out for him. You plugged the culvert causing the water to rise. The two boys had driven across his lawn to get around the plugged ditch. You knew he would be out there that morning on his wagon, waiting for them. The switched medication made him lethargic. A push on the wagon and he rolls into the water and drowns. Not very imaginative."

"Carmine was an old man. I figured no one would question a simple accident."

"The call from Phoenix must have come as quite a surprise. After twenty years as a respectable member of this community the *Don* calls in the chit." Titus watched Anthony's face turn sour.

"I should have known it would never have been forgotten." He took a deep breath shaking his head softly. "Carmine was angry. If the Riverview Corporation dumped the Sun Dancer he would be out his only income. He figured to get even. Or maybe just threaten. At any rate, some people, powerful people, couldn't take the chance that his memoirs would be made public."

Titus was focused on the gun Anthony was holding. "So a call came for Angelo DeGostini. That's you. That's how you came to Lawrence. Twenty-five years ago you helped set up a New York brokerage house for a takeover by the Bonanno family. In return you were set up here with enough money to go into the banking business. Part of the deal was you were to keep track of Carmine Valentino. He was loyal to Vincient Peretti, but there were people who were worried he knew things that they didn't want made public. People with important names. Recently he had a visitor. A young woman from a New York publishing house. Word had gotten to the mob that he had written about the old days and named names."

Very slowly Anthony brought the gun around and laid it in his lap covering it with his left hand.

"It took some doing, and I had some help," Titus went on. "But we found the manuscript."

Anthony's face flashed curiosity.

Of Mourning Doves and Heroes

"It was in a weatherproof box in the Japanese lantern. The only thing not destroyed when you torched the house."

Anthony began rocking back and forth slowly as Titus continued. "When Dallas Massley started asking questions about this Angelo Degostini, he was killed. Tony's deal with the Sun Dancer just happened to come along and muddle things up. He tried to scare Ann Marie, then got desperate and jimmied my furnace. Maybe he put some things together. Like getting out of that jam at the police academy. It must have surprised him to find out that his easygoing, well-respected father had enough pull with the right people to get him out of a situation like that."

Their eyes were locked together. Titus' relaxed a bit. When he looked down he felt his heart stop, Anthony's gun was pointed at him. "Don't do this, Anthony. It won't help. Three people are dead already."

Anthony's voice was strangely distant. "I had put the Bonannos and the Perettis so far back in my memory it was like it was someone else. This is my home, Ty. Lawrence. I know almost everybody in the county by name. Many I call friends."

The dull sheen in his eyes changed. They were brighter. "I never thought I would ever hear from them again, but I did. They made it clear the pact I had made twenty-five years ago was guaranteed with my life. Now I've lost everything. Including my son."

He picked a framed photograph off the desk and stared at it. Then set it down. On it Titus could see a man and woman dressed as he and Sandra had looked on their wedding day.

"I've stared at this gun all afternoon, Ty. But I don't have the guts." As Anthony's voice trailed off his shoulders sagged. He looked like he was getting smaller. "I can tell you I'm not going with you," he said, lifting his head.

Titus measured his words. "Just put the gun down. Sheriff Watkins will be here any minute."

Anthony grinned. "No. You think it's over but it's not. You see, you're going to do it for me."

Titus felt a heat settle over him. "No way, Anthony."

Anthony lowered his gun slightly. "This is the way it's going to be, you see. I am going to shoot you in the leg, count to five then shoot you in the belly. I'm betting you won't let me get the second shot off."

Titus' hands began to shake. His ears picked out the faint wail of a siren. "Don't do this Anthony."

Anthony's shoulders straightened, his lips moved.

"Noooooooo!!!" Titus' shout roared through his head as the fiery blow smashed through his left thigh, tearing his leg from under him, spinning him hard against the wall. He twisted around facing Anthony, his left hand clutching at the fire searing in his leg. He locked his right leg tight to stay on his feet. Time slowed to a near stop. He watched a grimace harden Anthony's face, saw the gun move left and center on him. His right knee gave a little, then buckled and he began to slip down the wall. To kill or be killed. Not the noble hero, killing to save an innocent. This was the primitive fight to live. Instinct.

A dark edge was narrowing his vision. He picked out the third button of Anthony's silk shirt, tightened his grip on the gun and squeezed the trigger.

Anthony slumped forward then tumbled from the desk before Titus allowed himself to crumple to the floor. A dark wall was closing. Blood was flowing through his fingers. He forced his eyes to stay open, heard JoAnna frantically calling his name, then saw her face come close as a curtain of blackness closed over him.

Ross Tarry

-17-

I t was the end of the in-between season. The time between winter and spring. When the danger of icy sidewalks is past. The sun, warmer and closer, caresses the skin with gentle tenderness. When the air carries the exhilarating fragrance of things coming back to life; grass greening, daffodils flowering and maple buds opening, revealing millions of delicate, miniature leaves.

The teapot whistled and Titus stepped back inside leaving the balcony doors open. In the kitchen he dumped a teaspoon of coffee crystals into one cup and dropped a teabag into another, then added scalding water from the pot and stirred. He had hooked a finger through the handle when he felt JoAnna's hands glide up his back.

"I like seeing you like this, dressed only in your trousers," she said in a soft lusty voice. Her arms slipped around him. Her breath was warm on his skin as she rested her face between his shoulders. Her familiar scent worked its magic, stirring him. He knew there would be no way he would ever be able to erase it from his memory. He set the tea on the counter and turned in her arms, feeling the frilly nightgown brush against his skin, then pushed back letting his gaze slowly slide down to her painted toes, then back up, lingering here and there until he met her eyes. "Let's take our cups back to bed."

"I can't. I have to open the gift shop by noon. Sunday is the museum's busiest day, you know. You wouldn't believe all the children."

The crystal clock on the mantel read nine-forty. His hands slid up her arms. He shifted his weight to his right leg. "How am I doing?" he asked, with hesitation.

"Doing?"

"You know. Expressing how I feel?"

She smiled and touched a finger to a corner of his mouth. "You've come a ways."

A curt grin tugged at his lips. "You are right, you know." He tapped his chest with his fingers. "There's a very secure feeling in here when you know where you stand with the one you love."

"I read a poem recently about friends, partners, and lovers. I'll have to see if I can find it." Her finger slipped over his lips. "But now I have to get ready. I have oodles of junk to sell."

"Here take your tea," he said, holding the cup with the handle pointed outward. "I'll get dressed and be out of here."

She came close and kissed his lips. "See you Friday then?"

Here she was only inches from him, yet the thought of their next time together sent his blood racing. "Yes," he whispered, planting a kiss delicately on her lips.

Her hands came up between them and she gently pushed. "Enough. Enough."

He released his arms reluctantly. It was always like this when it was time to let her go.

JoAnna was half way down the hall when he remembered. "Jo, Ann Marie has been working on the Seabring case. The child abuse case. It goes to trial Wednesday and she'll be handling the prosecution. Her first courtroom work since she's been back. I told her I'd be in the gallery. Would you like to come with me?"

"Yes. I'm scheduled at the hospital, but I can get out of it."

"It's not necessary to change your plans."

"Oh yes it is. It's important that I be there with you. Besides, by Wednesday I'm beginning to miss you already."

*   *   *

Titus held JoAnna's hand as the two left the elevator and walked to the courtroom at the far end of the hall. He held the shiny black cane in his left hand and pushed the heavy oak door open with the other.

In the jury box eight women and four men sat as unmoving as mannequins, anchored in their seats by the weight of responsibility. Ann Marie was at the prosecutor's table studying a folder, her wheelchair shunted to the far-left corner behind a bailiff. At the table to her right a well-groomed young man was staring at the oak wall behind the judge's bench. Beside him a man in a gray suit poured over a sheaf of papers. A rustling of whispers emanated from the first three rows of people outside the oak banister. The gallery, the last four rows of wood benches, was empty except for Cliff Hensley seated on the end in the second row.

Cliff turned and started to rise when he saw JoAnna and Titus. Titus put his hand on the deputy's shoulder as JoAnna slipped into the first bench. "This will be fine," he said, easing himself down beside her, hooking his cane over the back of the bench in front of him. The muscles of his neck tightened, a hard thought passed through his mind. From here he could see the glint of the steel brace below the cuff of Ann Marie's left pant leg. The device of straps and steel rods, from the sole of her foot to her thigh, allowed her to sit by unlocking at the knee. They both had mastered walking again over the past months. For him it was a matter of allowing the torn thigh muscle to mend the best it could. For Ann Marie it had been a more difficult struggle. But she had mastered the contraption with bulldog tenacity.

He forced the muscles in his neck to relax. Justice, most times, doesn't atone for the crime. No matter how it's meted out, it leaves a feeling of unfinished business.

He leaned forward. "Is she nervous?" he whispered into Cliff's ear.

Cliff shook his head. "You know her. If she says she's going to do something, she'll do it."

JoAnna's half smile turned Titus' head. "Just like her father," she mouthed softly.

He jabbed her tenderly on the leg, grinned and leaned back.

"All rise!" The sharp call of the bailiff quieted the courtroom as the judge came briskly through the corner door, climbed to his seat, said a few words to the jury then nodded in the direction of Ann Marie.

Titus watched as Ann Marie straightened in her chair, pressed her hands against the tabletop and pushed herself to her feet. Steadying herself with her fingertips she turned to face the jury box. He could see the determination set in hard lines across her face. She took a tentative step then moved with an awkward gait across the courtroom to the jury box.

Titus saw her right hand clamp to the oak banister. He watched as she carefully scanned each juror, her hand tightly gripping the oak bar.

"Ladies and Gentlemen," she said, in her clear professional voice. "We met earlier this morning when you were selected to be on this jury, but I am going to reintroduce my self. My name is Ann Marie Closson. I work for the Benson County Prosecutor's office. It is my job to present the state's case against the defendant, Mr. Gerald Seabring. I will do this by introducing witnesses, and presenting evidence that will prove to you that Mr. Seabring did on October twelfth of last year, brutally beat then murder his four-year-old stepson, Kyle Branson, by dropping him off a second story balcony."

Titus unhooked the cane from the back of the bench, propped it up between his legs with both hands and pulled his shoulders back. Though a smile felt inappropriate for these proceedings, it came. Unchecked.

The End

Of Mourning Doves and Heroes

TO ORDER COPIES OF THIS BOOK

SEND $12.99 TO

KIELEY PUBLISHING
P. O. Box 58 ST.MICHAEL, MN 55376
OR GO TO gennykieleybooks.com

While you're there check out these other Novels from
KIELEY PUBLISHING
and NIGHT WRITERS.

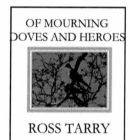

Nightmares and Dreams
By Lyn Miller LaCoursiere
300 Pages............$12.99

Of Mourning Doves
and Heroes
By Ross Tarry
208 Pages.....$12.99

Coming Soon
Cardinal Red, Last Cry of the Whipporwill,
Sunsets, Tomorrow's Rain, and Suddenly Summer.

**Make sure to include your name, address
with city, state & zip code.
Add $2.50 for postage on each book.**